Praise f

THE BRI

"*The Bridge* is an absorbing human drama complete with romantic undercurrents and spiritual eddies. Written with a deft hand, it will introduce you to people you will want as friends and to a country setting so breathtaking you won't want to leave. This is one of those novels you don't just read, you live it."

—JACK CAVANAUGH, *best-selling author*

"I have only one complaint about *The Bridge*—once you pick it up, you can't put it down, no matter how much you might need to sleep or perform other essential daily functions. This is a masterfully told, riveting story about characters so real you'll be carrying on conversations with them weeks after you finish the book. Read it. Let it engage your imagination, warm your heart, and ignite your faith. But when you find yourself sleep-deprived and carrying on conversations with imaginary people, don't say I didn't warn you."

—CAROLYN ARENDS, *recording artist and author*

"Lisa Tawn Bergren spreads a banquet fit for story-lovers in *The Bridge*. This story of hope, honor, and love provides a feast of imagery from the opening scene all the way through. This is Bergren at her best. Don't be surprised if you find yourself weeping on the last page even while you smile."

—ROBIN JONES GUNN, *best-selling author*

"In *The Bridge,* Lisa Tawn Bergren has written a tender story of love—the love between a man and a woman, the love between a father and his son, and the love God showers upon us all. It's a story that will linger in your heart long after the last page is read."

—ROBIN LEE HATCHER, *best-selling author*

THE
BRIDGE

THE
BRIDGE

 a Novel

LISA TAWN
BERGREN

WATERBROOK
PRESS

THE BRIDGE
PUBLISHED BY WATERBROOK PRESS
2375 Telstar Drive, Suite 160
Colorado Springs, CO 80920
A division of Random House, Inc.

ISBN 1-57856-536-7

Library of Congress Cataloging-in-Publication Data
Bergren, Lisa Tawn.
    The bridge / by Lisa Tawn Bergren.—1st ed.
      p.   cm.
    ISBN 1-57856-536-7 (pbk.)
      1. Traffic accident victims—Family relationships—Fiction. 2. Fathers and sons—Fiction.
    3. Mothers—Death—Fiction. 4. Montana—Fiction. I. Title

PS3552.E71938 B75 2000
813'.54—dc 21

                                                                00-043543

Printed in the United States of America
2002

10 9 8 7 6 5 4 3

To Timothy

husband, lover, friend

on the river forever with me

ACKNOWLEDGMENTS

The Bridge was first inspired by Gary Chapman's "Sweet Jesus," a song that moves me to tears to this day. It grew from there. Many thanks to my readers, who caught innumerable mistakes and made many solid suggestions to help make this what I hope is my best book yet: Erin Healy, Liz Curtis Higgs, Diane Noble, Monica Bryant, Tricia Goyer (who also helped with on-site research), Rebecca Price, Don Pape, and Danya Clairmont. Ruth and Joe McKay met me at Glacier International Airport to send me off with information on trees indigenous to the area. My editors, Traci DePree and Penelope Stokes, did remarkable work. My dad dared to take me fly-fishing; my mom canvassed the Swan with me. Their love and support over the years has been unfailing. The Lord is good indeed.

We've become disillusioned, disheartened,
apathetic people because we've lost the ability
to experience enchantment, wonder and awe.

THOMAS MOORE

PROLOGUE

July 1961

Ernie Powell smiled in satisfaction as he closed the cabin's creaking screen door behind him. He took a deep breath of the Swan River morning. There was no place like northwest Montana in July, and today was proof of it.

He reached for his forty-year-old fly rod and made his way to the riverbank, admiring the view before him as he would a treasured old friend. There was always something familiar yet startlingly unique about the river. This morning, a thin layer of fog hovered just above the still pools created by piles of logs, generating an unearthly golden glow above deep green water. Here and there, boulders were beginning to emerge from waters that were waning from their snowmelt zenith to the more subdued levels of midsummer.

About twenty-five yards downstream was Ernie's favorite fishing spot, near the old bridge he had watched them build when he was just a boy. The trout favored the logjam's shadows that shielded them from the rising sun and were often hungry at this time in the morning. Although the air was cool, he could tell the fog would soon be gone. It would be a warm day.

With rubber boots on, he waded in until the river reached midcalf. The icy waters licked at his bones, making ankles and knees—too old to walk a mile—ache in protest. He smiled again. Ernie liked the challenge of the river, her silent shout to turn and leave the fish alone. *Not a chance, old girl.* Martha was planning on trout for breakfast, and after sixty-some years of marriage, he knew better than to disappoint her.

Ernie reached into the basket at his hip, studying the flow of the river as he pulled out and attached his fly—hand tied just the night before—to the line, then cast it out to the sweet spot the fish favored. The blue-and-green Spanner was just floating down past the deepest pool when he heard a car approaching. Odd, he thought, at this hour. It was early for any traffic. He grumbled under his breath. Vibrations from traffic scared away the trout.

He hated the increasing number of automobiles that passed over the rickety old wooden bridge, but growth was inevitable, he supposed. The other side of the river now had more than eighteen cabins. Fifty years ago only he and the Conways had places along this part of the Swan. With so much traffic, the county would have to get to replacing the old bridge soon. Why, even from where he stood, with eyes that weren't what they used to be, Ernie could see the rot that ate at the pilings.

Ernie muttered under his breath. He had missed his opportunity over the deep pool. He pulled in his line and cast again as the car left the gravel above him and began crossing the one-lane bridge. Planks creaked, and the entire bridge moaned under the weight. Ernie frowned. This was a different sound than its usual protest. What was ordinarily a *chu-chunk chu-chunk* was now a keening, splitting scream.

The car had just made it to the center of the bridge when Ernie heard the *crack* of a thousand broken bones and watched in horror as a central piling collapsed. "Oh no," he muttered under his breath. The next piling went too. "God in heaven…no!"

The silver Buick slipped backward into the sudden crevasse, and Ernie heard a woman scream. He dropped his rod and shouted, not knowing what he said, too stunned to move. The back of the Buick hit the water with a tremendous splash, buoyed for a moment, then started sinking impossibly fast, the front still sticking upward. A baby wailed. As the woman kept shrieking, a cross section fell from the bridge, crashing through the windshield. The shrieking stopped. But the baby's cry went on, increasingly furious.

Without another thought, Ernie pulled off his boots and stumbled downriver, wincing as rocks bit into his tender flesh. He had not been swimming for nearly twenty years, but he did not hesitate. He ran into the water, watching as the car yanked against the bridge that held it, flooding as the river urged it downstream. When the water reached his waist, Ernie dived in, gasping at the cold that took his breath away. *Dear Father,* he prayed again as he made his way to the wreck, shuddering as the cold chilled his flesh, *dear God in heaven, please let me help them. I'm just an old man. Give me the strength…*

His gnarled hand grasped at the driver's side of the car, and he carefully hauled himself upward to look through the broken windshield, conscious of the precarious hold the decrepit bridge had on the Buick. What he saw inside took his breath away faster than the cold. A young woman, her face under water, her body pinned beneath the rotting wood sticking through the windshield, fixed upon him with desperate eyes. Ernie saw blood pool in the water around her waist and filter away like fiery sunset clouds in a strong wind.

She held the baby above her, frantically trying to keep him safe, and his bright red face turned toward Ernie. His fury startled the old man back into breathing.

Ernie glanced at the woman, wondering how to get them out, and her eyes told him everything.

He could not save them both.

She was handing him her child, her love, for him to save. The car groaned, and the mother slipped farther under, bubbles that signaled the last breath she would ever take rising to the surface. Swallowing hard, Ernie grabbed the babe from her icy, trembling fingers and watched in horror as they sank. He cast himself away from the wreck, sobbing, holding the child above water until he came back up himself, then resting the boy on his chest as he swam, swam with everything in him for the shore.

Dear God, it's cold, he prayed to the Savior who had long been his friend. *Please let me get this child to the shore. If I can do this one last thing...*

His heart pounded painfully against his ribs, and Ernie wondered for the first time if he would survive. The babe quieted. Probably going into shock, Ernie assessed distantly, remembering soldiers in trenches during the Great War. There was a bright light, and Ernie wondered why the sun was so high in the sky at this early hour. He felt rocks beneath him, and he stumbled to his feet, desperate for a foothold. His arms were falling asleep, and Ernie struggled to hold on to the baby. It was bright, so bright...

Ernie collapsed onto the mud and grass of the Swan's bank one last time. He inhaled the sweet, mossy scent, felt the long river reeds on his cheek and the life squirming on his chest. The light was too intense for him to see much, but there was a man beside him then, a powerful giant of a man, and Ernie was glad, so glad that help had arrived. "The child—"

"The child is well," said the man kindly. "And you will be too. I am proud of you, Ernie. Now come. Come with me."

Rick climbed into bed with her, throwing an arm around her swollen waistline.

"Where've you been?" she whispered. "I was worried."

"Everywhere, baby. Nowhere special."

"You told me we were going to talk tonight, Rick."

"I did?" he mumbled sleepily. "'Bout what?"

"Yes. About getting married." She sat up, giving in to her frustration. "This baby's due any day, Rick. Are you going to be his father or what?"

"Anna, I'm beat. Can we talk about this tomorrow?"

"That's what you say every day. Tomorrow. Every day you say tomorrow. I want to talk about it now."

He sat up too, his brow furrowing over frightful green eyes. "Anna, I've got a killer headache. We'll talk about it. Soon. Now go to sleep."

Irritated but cowed by the angry look on his face, Anna chose to lay back down on her side, facing away from him. Angrily she tucked the covers around her.

He was never going to marry her. Who was she kidding anyway?

CHAPTER ONE

June 10, 2000

"Oh, c'mon!" Jared Conway yelled, hitting the leather-covered dashboard of his new BMW. Some idiot ahead had double-parked his rig and left it, blocking a whole lane of traffic. The New Yorkers on his left couldn't have cared less—they weren't letting one more car in ahead of *them*.

"No, not you, Don," he said, speaking into his car phone. "It's this blasted traffic. It's as bad as I've seen."

"Listen to me, Conway. We've gotta move. Our cotton contracts are down three percent. If we don't sell now, we're gonna lose."

"No. Let's keep it in play. Something'll happen to the Russians' cotton too. We might be facing a drought, but they'll get locusts *and* a drought. I can feel it. Let's hold on. "

There was silence on the other end. "Don?"

"We're gonna risk fifty thousand on another one of your *feelings?*"

"My company, my call. Call me back in an hour and give me a status on those percentage points."

"I'm a junior partner in that company, and we still gotta talk coffee."

"I'll take mine black, one sugar."

"Funny—"

"Don, my cell phone's ringing. Hold on." Jared took a moment to lay on his horn, then set the car phone down to pick up his cellular. He made an angry gesture toward a woman who was carefully ignoring his attempt to edge into her lane.

"Conway," he answered.

"Mr. Jared Conway?"

"That's me."

"This is Julie Vose, calling from Bigfork, Montana."

"Yeah. What can I do for you, Ms. Vose?"

She paused. "I'm the real estate agent who called last month. You had said you were interested in selling your uncle's cabin?"

"Oh yeah, yeah. Sorry. I'm a little distracted right now."

"Yes, well, I did go by the cabin. It's in good structural shape, could be a real gem with a little cosmetic work, but it's chock full."

"Of what?"

"Of stuff. Your uncle was something of a pack rat, Mr. Conway. In the cabin, on the grounds…everywhere. There's a ton of material made for a garage sale."

"Uncle Rudy?"

"Yes. The neighbors tell me that if one didn't feel like going all the way to town, they would run by Rudy's to see if he had a spare."

"Spare what?"

"Spare anything. Mr. Conway, there is simply too much for me to take care of. You'll need to come and clean the place out before I can sell it."

Jared groaned. "Can't we hire someone?"

"Well, of course. We could. But there might be some things

you'd care to keep in there. Somebody else can't really make those kinds of decisions for you."

Jared's attention was drawn to his car phone, on its side in the passenger seat, where he could hear Don yelling at the top of his lungs. He picked it up and held it to his other ear. "Don."

"It went down again, Jared!"

"Hold on, Don. Do *not* sell."

"Ms. Vose? Give me your number. I'll call you back." He scribbled it on his mounted notepad on the dash as Don droned on in his other ear. "Thanks. I'll call you soon."

"Tomorrow?" she pressed.

"I'll do my best." He pressed the "end" button, cutting her off, and returned to the car phone.

"Conway! This is my money too!"

"Yeah, Don, but more mine than yours. I said hold. Do not sell." He hung up on his best friend with a grin. Eighty percent of the time Jared was right when he went with his gut instinct. If he was wrong, he'd make it up to Don soon enough. If he was right, Don would be buying dinner.

He took a deep breath and let it out slowly. It seemed he could do his work in his sleep these days. The only thing fun about it anymore was when he could bait Don and watch for his reaction.

Jared sighed in relief as the lane-blocking truck driver returned, climbed into the cab, and put his rig into gear, waving cheerily as if Jared had greeted him with a friendly grin. Jared laughed under his breath, too tired to be angry anymore. Now all he wanted was a quiet evening with Patricia and a chance to pack for their trip. Tomorrow they'd pick up their son at the boarding school and decide where to go on vacation, a vacation two years overdue. He glanced at his watch, his grin growing wider. With any luck he'd still be home a half-hour early. He couldn't remember when he'd ever been early arriving home.

Twelve blocks later he turned and entered a quiet side street. He missed this neighborhood, these old haunts. The big oaks that towered overhead, intermingling limbs. The neatly kept three-story buildings, tightly packed together yet each distinct. There was a wonderful fresh-produce grocer across the street and an ancient used-books store down the block. If things continued to go well with Patricia and they were able to reconcile and remarry, he could move back into his beloved old flat. Maybe they could even bring Nicolaus back home for good, be a family... He eased into a narrow parking spot and slammed the door, leaving his briefcase behind as the alarm *che-cheeped* in response to the button on his keys.

He quickly jogged up the brick-and-cement stairs to the heavy front door and glanced at his watch again. The extra effort to extricate himself from the office had paid off. Stuck in traffic but still half an hour early! Maybe he'd make it a habit if it made Patricia happy. Yes, it would be good to be home. And to see Patricia.

The new key—given to him just a week prior—slipped into the lock as he pictured his ex-wife dressed for dinner. They were going out to celebrate tonight. One last evening alone before Nick was with them. He'd asked her to wear her black linen dress, and he could already see those long, shapely legs meeting a short skirt, narrow waist, and curvaceous top. Nearly as tall as he without heels and with long, straight, white-blond hair, Patricia was certain to turn every head at the restaurant. And once again he would play the part of the happy suitor. Maybe if things went well, a fantastic dinner for two would seal things for her. Convince her it was time to give him, their marriage, another chance. He was banking on it as surely as he was the Russians' cotton failure.

He trudged up the stairs, ignoring the sounds of an argument between the couple who lived in the flat beneath them. He only wanted to think about happy things now—how he and Patricia would go pick up Nick, tell him he was coming home again, tell him they were going to remarry. The boy would be ecstatic. If only he hadn't pushed for the divorce three years ago! Sure, she had slipped into an affair, but it wasn't as if the wounds couldn't be healed. He was ready to forgive, to move on and make a real go of it. Fumbling with his keys, he finally found the right one, turned it in the deadbolt of the front door, and let himself in.

Patricia stood near the couch, a false smile lighting up her face as she pushed back her disheveled hair, even as she finished pulling on the cardigan of a gold sweater set. "Jared, darling! You're home early!"

Surprised by her look of covert panic, Jared's eyes moved to the bedroom—the bedroom they had once shared—where dancing shadows told him she was not alone. "Who's that?" he asked, deadly still, his heart dropping. He held his breath as he slipped the keys into his pants pocket.

But the bare-chested young man appeared, placing a hand on either side of the bedroom doorway and lopping Patricia a lazy smile, before she could answer. "Company?"

"My ex-husband," she said lightly.

"Get out," Jared ordered.

"Jared—"

"I can't believe you've done this again."

"What? I've—"

"No, Patricia. This is it. We're done." He shook his head slightly, amazed at his own stupidity. "You've destroyed everything we've tried to rebuild."

"You don't understand. Eric's just a friend—"

"No, *you* don't understand. We're through. Don't tell me he's just a friend. You and I both know what was going on here." He sat down heavily on the leather sofa. "I've given you everything I had, and it's still not enough. I thought we'd changed, you'd changed, that I—I don't know what you want. Maybe that man does," he said, hooking a thumb over his shoulder toward the front door as Eric eagerly departed, tugging his shirt on as he went. "I'm through guessing. I'm through trying."

She sank onto the sofa opposite him, the glass coffee table between them. The smile had vanished. "So that's it. After all we've been through."

The accusation in her voice brought Jared's anger forward. "Yes, that's it! You just sealed the deal." He rose. "I was ready to give us another chance, Patricia. But I told you the one thing—the *one* thing—I couldn't bear would be another affair. This is your doing. Not mine." He turned away from her then, amazed that her perfect features suddenly seemed cold, harsh, rather than alluring. "I'm going to pick up Nick," he said over his shoulder. "He and I will take a short vacation. I'll break the news to him that we're not gonna make it." He paused, waiting for any complaint, but she remained silent.

A day later, Jared pulled into the long, oak-lined drive of Buckley Boys' Academy. The two hundred-year-old grounds brought back happy memories of Jared's own boyhood days, but he still had hoped to give his children a home at home. He had given in to Patricia's pushing as usual. The truth was she was tired of being a full-time mother, and the social prestige of getting into the expensive school hadn't hurt her ego either. He would never forget the look on Nicolaus's face when Jared told his then five-year-old that they were sending him away to school—disbelief, betrayal, disappointment, fear. Nick had adapted well in the last three years at the academy, excelling in both mathematics and field hockey, but the look on his face when they dropped him off that first day still plagued Jared.

Still, this school was one of the best; posh, clean, good faculty, and a Christian history that urged brief nods toward its faith foundations by demanding weekly worship in the chapel. Jared himself was strictly a Christmas and Easter kind of believer, but he fondly remembered the dear old Episcopalian priest who had been at the school when he was a student. Father Frank had had a sparkle in his eye, a bounce to his step, and always seemed completely at ease with himself. At eighty he still served as the school's rector. The image of the kindly priest brought Jared up short; he hadn't thought of him in some time.

Nick was outside the main hall, hanging from an ancient tree above an impeccable lawn as other boys greeted family members and departed for the summer holiday. The child did not recognize his father's new car, so Jared parked in the nearest lot and watched him for a bit. It took a moment for Jared to realize why he was hesitating in retrieving the boy—there had been such hope in Nick's voice when Jared had told him that his mother and he were considering getting back together. Now he was about to dash that dream of a

Cleaver family reunion. Would he alone be enough for Nicolaus? Or would the boy rather have his mother?

Jared tried to swallow, but his mouth was dry. Taking a deep breath, he opened the car door and strode across the parking lot toward his son. Nicolaus was upright now, sitting on a fat branch, watching the countless other families, occasionally looking down the road for his own. He was a handsome kid. People said he was the spitting image of his father, which made Jared quite proud. The same dark hair, the green eyes, the cut of his chin…

"Nick!" Jared's voice sounded unnaturally bright.

"Dad!" the boy turned toward him and jumped down, then ran, stumbling over a tree root, then pushing on, ecstatic to see his father. "Dad!" he said again, jumping into Jared's arms. After a brief, fierce hug, Jared set him down.

"Where's Mom?"

Jared glanced at the ground, kicking at another root. He forced himself to meet his son's look. "She's at home, Nicolaus. She isn't coming."

"At all? On our vacation?"

Jared shook his head, placing a reassuring hand on his son's shoulder.

Nicolaus glumly pulled on his backpack straps and then picked up his two duffel bags, the crisp, formal Buckley insignia monogrammed on one side, his initials on the other.

Jared guided him away from the nearest family, the perfect family—father, mother, daughter, two sons in Buckley uniforms. Why couldn't Patricia have seen the importance, the beauty of it? Why'd she have to go and trash all of his dreams, and Nick's too? "Your mother's got other plans. Come here." He sat down on a wrought-iron bench and urged Nick to do so too, but the boy refused. "Nick, we tried to get back together, but it didn't work. I'm sorry. We've called it quits again." When his son didn't respond, Jared adopted a lighter tone. "So it's just you and me. I promise it won't be so bad."

"Can we go?"

"Sure," Jared said slowly, spotting the hint of tears for the first time. "Want me to carry—"

"No. I got it," the boy said gruffly. All traces of joy were gone, crushed in the wake of his mother's absence. Jared sneaked another look at him, noticing changes, evidence of maturation. He was growing up. Fast. It made Jared worry that he had already missed too much. There was a hardened pain in the clench of the boy's jaw, a tired worry in the corner of his eye that reminded Jared of his own image in the mirror. The boy had already inherited his looks; now he was inheriting his pain.

Nick threw his bags into the trunk of the BMW, not even commenting on his father's new car. He slumped to the passenger-side door and dropped inside. Jared did the same on the driver's side, then quickly cranked the engine to get the air conditioning going. The humidity in upstate New York was already outrageous.

"So, where we goin'?" Nick asked dully. The ache in the boy's voice made Jared want to take him to Europe, do anything to distract him, if it would ease the agony.

"Anywhere. I'm packed; you're packed. The Great Lakes? Grand Canyon? We could go camping! There's Florida and Disney World. Or we could take old Route 66…"

"What's Route 66?"

"An old highway down south." Jared cast about for a few more alternatives, willing Nicolaus to see the lengths he would go to to make him feel better. "We could hop a plane for Germany…or the Bahamas!"

Nick remained silent.

Sighing, Jared glanced from the boy, along the dashboard, to his own window. Pausing, his eyes retraced their path to the number on his notepad. "What about Montana? My uncle died last winter and left me an old cabin on a river. I have to go empty it out. It's not—"

"You mean it?" Nick asked, eyes wide, practically bouncing in his seat. "A cabin in Montana? Can we go fishing? Go hiking? I have a friend who went fishing last year with his dad, and he said it was cool." His face fell.

"What?"

"I don't have a pole."

Jared smiled and pulled out his Rand McNally map, looking for the *M* states. "That, my boy, I can fix. Let's go to Montana, and I'll buy you a pole. Heck, I'll buy myself a pole, and we'll fish together." He opened the map and gave a low whistle.

"What?"

"Montana's a big state. And quite a drive. It'll take us three, maybe four days. Still up for it?"

"Yes!"

Jared sighed and then put the BMW into gear. *Why not?* he asked himself. He had plenty of vacation time, and there wasn't anything he'd rather do at the moment than spend time with Nicolaus. Besides, he'd empty out Uncle Rudy's cabin and be done with it, a hundred thousand richer for his efforts when it sold.

When the nurse discharged her three days after her son's birth, Anna wearily gathered their things together—a change of clothing, the hospital's gift of a thin baby blanket and cap, a few cloth diapers, and her toiletries—then looked around the room. She was loathe to leave the clean, quiet place, afraid that bringing the baby home to Rick might not do all she dreamed for them—make them a family at long last.

Anna glanced at her watch and then moved a little faster. The bus would be outside any minute, and if she and her son were to get home before dark, they would need to make this connection. A part of her had hoped that Rick would borrow a friend's car and pick them up, but she understood that was a foolish dream. After all, he hadn't even stopped at the hospital to visit since the night she went into labor. He was just busy at his new job; that was it. Working hard to provide for his new family.

A nurse walked in then, smiling and cooing over the baby in her arms. She handed him to Anna, saying, "Take good care of that baby boy. And yourself. Let us know if you have any questions once you get home."

"I will," Anna promised.

CHAPTER TWO

Eden Powell awakened before daybreak, the image of her trouble-some dream etched into her soul. She could still see the woman in the dim light, cowering on the floor, one hand covering her neck, the other stretched before her. Eden couldn't remember the rest of the dream, but she couldn't get the figure out of her mind.

Sighing, she rose and pulled on a sweatshirt and sweatpants, slipped her feet into woolen mules, then tied back her hair, still sleep-messy, into a knot. The familiarity of years allowed her to walk in the dark, out of her small cottage to the storage shed. She opened the creaking wooden door and reached for the twine tied to the bare bulb's chain high above. Light flooded the small outbuilding.

To one side was finished pottery, waiting to be glazed. On the other were supplies. In back was her giant kiln, a gift from her mother. Professional in size and quality, it had changed Eden's life, directed the course of her work. A ceramist by trade, she loved the soothing work of molding plates and pots and cups, but images such as the one in her dream nagged at her, begged for her to sculpt them from clay. Once again the alarming mental picture of the woman came to mind. She had learned long ago that her creative inspiration came from the depth and breadth of life, and placing her visions and dreams and insights on that life into clay was a therapeutic and freeing process. In truth, she couldn't wait to get to the woman from her dreams.

She pulled a five-pound block of raw Montana clay from the shelf, and then another. After five trips to the storage shed, she shut the door and returned to the covered porch on which she had begun to work. Summer was well on its way, though the mornings were still crisp and the days not hot. It encouraged her to work there instead of in her attic studio, which she found winter-stale and spring-claustrophobic.

Quickly Eden set down a plywood sheet. On it she arranged a wire foundation in the general configuration of the woman in her mind. She moved the blocks alongside the mesh mold. Then going back into the house for a bowl of warm water, she started coffee and slipped into her barn jacket, shivering a little. She opened the porch door again, looking for a hint of daybreak. It was still quite dark, but the sounds of awakening morning welcomed her—the tentative warble of a vireo, the heavy lake waves striking shore, the rustling of the trees as they swayed in the stiff southwest breeze. The wind was common to the Swan at this hour, often washing over the valley from the peaks south of the lake, over the southern river that dumped into it, along the length of its eleven miles, then down and beyond the northern river that led past Eden's great-grandparents' cabin and onward to town.

She flipped on an overhead light switch, wincing at the glare.

After pressing handfuls of clay together across the mesh formation, she lowered her hands to the chipped, white enamel bowl that had belonged to her grandmother, appreciating the warmth of the water. Dropping to her knees, she set to work, kneading a curve here, cutting away an angle there. She loved the feel of the cold clay under her fingers, the wet slip that reminded her of making mud pies with her brother when they were children. Gradually the dream image took shape as the sun warmed the eastern sky and then climbed to crest the mountains down the lake.

If the sounds of a car hadn't interrupted her, Eden didn't know when she would have stopped. A door slammed, and Eden looked up to see her friend Renee Scott walking toward her. Caught, she had no time to cover the "troubled woman," as she came to call the figure. She leaned back, grimacing at the stiffness in her legs and the pain in her knees from kneeling for so long.

Eden watched as Renee spotted her on her knees before the sculpture. Renee paused, her eyes going from Eden to the project before her. "Good morning," she managed. She climbed the two steps to the covered porch door, still staring through the screening at the clay.

"Good morning," Eden said softly.

"Early morning inspiration, eh?"

"Could say that. Come in. Want a cup of coffee?"

"Sure."

"I don't know how warm it is."

"That's okay. I just came by to pick up…" She let the screen door slam behind her as she studied the clay figure. "Eden, she's *incredible.*"

Eden sniffed, as if blowing off her praise, but her friend's words secretly warmed her. "Just one of those God images. Something I had to get into clay to get it out of my mind."

Renee seemed enraptured as she walked around the figure, examining, admiring. "What's she hiding from? What's scaring her?"

"I don't know." Eden rose and turned toward the door that led into the cottage. "I don't have any cream. Milk okay?"

"Fine, fine," Renee said, waving in her direction. "I've never seen you work in this scale before."

"No. Not since college. Her image woke me up this morning. She just had to be...big."

"She's perfect." Renee lifted her face, clearly awed. It embarrassed Eden.

"As I said, just one of those things I had to get out my head."

Renee followed her into the kitchen. "It's called muse, Eden. Inspiration."

"A flighty, artsy thing," Eden finished for her. She poured two mugs of lukewarm coffee.

"Hardly." Renee frowned.

Eden turned away, fighting off the urge to squirm under her friend's gaze. Renee had been pestering her for years to do more sculpture. "Toast?"

"Sure, but no butter. Eden, I want to sell her. Put her smack dab in the middle of my gallery."

"I don't think so." Eden shook her head.

"Why?"

"I don't know. She's not for sale. She's for me."

"You're going to keep her? Display her out here in the family room?"

"Probably not."

"I thought not. You'll hide her, like you do all the rest. When are you going to take a chance, Eden? Risk a little?"

"Maybe next year," Eden said, a teasing smile pulling up the corners of her lips.

"You laugh. But that's what you always say. 'Next year I'll go to Seattle with you. Next year I'll try two-step lessons.'" She came around the corner of the counter and took Eden's hands, her eyes pleading. "Ever since Todd..."

"Left me at the altar?"

"Yes. Ever since then you've refused to risk. If you would just live your life with all the passion you've poured into that sculpture outside, your life would look totally different."

Eden turned away from her and walked to the kitchen window. She gazed down the lake. "You don't know what it was like. How it felt."

"Oh, Eden. I was there."

"It's not the same thing, Renee. You were the maid of honor, not the bride." She turned back to her friend. "You weren't in a thousand-dollar wedding gown, with a hundred people sitting in the church."

"No. Brian waited until after we were married to tell me he didn't love me." Renee came close again and put her arm around Eden's shoulders. "I get the pain. I've had my own share," she said, referring to her divorce five years prior.

"At least you were spared the public humiliation." Even talking about it made Eden tremble with remembered agony. Never again. Never again would she allow such potential for pain in her life.

"I'm just worried about you, Eden. You have your whole life sewed up in this neat little sack—held together by your friends and family on one side, work on the other, and your faith in the middle." She sighed, letting her arm slip from Eden's shoulder. "But where is that faith, really? Why can't you try and trust again? You're almost thirty-five. Todd was a jerk and he hurt you, but that was twelve years ago. Just because he hurt you doesn't mean everyone else is waiting to do the same."

They stood together for a silent moment. Then Eden said, "You're here to pick up the plates."

"Don't switch the subject."

"I've got 'em all ready for you." She slid the cookie sheet with homemade walnut bread under the broiler of her narrow, white stove.

"We're talking about something important here."

"The plates are ready. And the bowls are almost done. I'll bring them in this afternoon."

Renee sighed and stared at Eden across the rim of her coffee mug.

"I think you'll like the glaze I chose. It's that river green color I was experimenting with. I'm sick to death of that iridescent glaze."

"It's still popular," Renee said. They both knew she was close to letting Eden off the hook.

"But I think they'll really go for this one." She checked on the toast, then closed the door for a moment more.

"I'm sure it will be very…serviceable."

"People like functional art."

"They like other kinds of art too."

Eden reached for a hot pad and then stared for a second at Renee. "You said no butter, right?"

"Right," Renee said, drawing out the word. "What about that art show in Seattle?"

"Maybe next year."

"Fine," she said, throwing up her hands. "You're missing out again."

"Pick me up a sweatshirt, will you?" Eden asked, going for her wallet. It was their way, these brief, fiery exchanges, then normal small talk. More the stuff of sisters than friends. Their conversation soon evolved to when Eden's parents planned to visit in July and how her brother was doing down in Missoula. It finished with the business at Renee's gallery.

When all that was left on their plates was crumbs and their coffee was drained, Renee stood. She checked her watch, which she always wore to the inside of her wrist, and whistled at the time. "Better get me those plates. I'll get your display set up, and you can bring me the bowls this afternoon."

Eden met her at the car and placed the packed box in the back. Renee unwrapped one and nodded. "That glaze will be a nice juxtaposition to those Asian reds and salmon pinks of the other ceramists' work." She ducked into the front of her Jeep, one leg still resting on the ground outside, and rolled down the window. "I didn't mean to lecture you, Eden. I just want you to take a risk once in a while, to be happy. If you—"

Eden sighed. "I *am* happy, Renee. You're meddling again."

Renee flashed her perfect, white teeth. "What are friends for? Remember, if you change your mind about going to Seattle, you can call me as late as 6:00 A.M. tomorrow, and I'll swing by to pick you up."

"6:00 A.M.," Eden dutifully repeated.

After dropping off the promised bowls that afternoon, Eden waved good-bye to Renee and walked out to Bigfork's main thoroughfare, Electric Avenue. Three blocks long, it was named for the dam at the south end of the street that held back the waters of the Swan and generated power for the valley. There were window boxes full of flowers, just now blooming. The storefronts had a western look, giving the town a quaint, touristy feel. But right now, before most of the summer people arrived, it belonged to the locals.

She took a deep breath and sighed in contentment. This place was paradise, home. And she didn't intend to risk upsetting the applecart for anything. She felt safe here. Secure. Peaceful.

Didn't people on the outside pay thousands of dollars to therapists, trying to reach this place—this tranquillity—inside? Renee was right; she didn't risk much. But she didn't feel a need to do so either. She smiled and headed across the quiet street to pick up a book from Sara, who ran the local bookstore. The vacationers had yet to arrive, but the store owners were raring to go. It had been a long, quiet winter in town, and they depended on the tourists for their income.

Sara Miller sat behind a big, old, wooden desk at the front of the store and smiled when Eden ducked in. With the healthy, welcoming look of her Eastern European ancestors and her friendly disposition, people were drawn to Sara. Like Renee, Sara shared Eden's passion for good art and music, good books and the outdoors. They'd been friends since elementary school.

"Did you get my book in?" Eden asked.

"Oh!" Sara said, her fingers splayed, eyes wide. "I'm glad you remembered! It came in yesterday." She swiveled in her chair and came back around with a copy of Ivan Doig's *Dancing at the Rascal Fair.* "I think you'll love it; it's set somewhere around the eastern slopes of Glacier."

"Great! What do I owe you?"

"Let's see. Ten even."

Eden dug in her backpack for her wallet, then handed over the money. "Where's the baby today?"

"Joe took her to the park. Sheridan was pretty excited."

"Looks like a nice day for it."

"Yeah," Sara said, wistfully looking out her window. "Wish I was off and could go for a hike."

"It's getting to be summer. You should start your routine of an early-morning hike."

"I was thinking the same thing. Somehow, though, with a kid, it's tough to get up in the morning."

"Come on, old lady. I'll meet you. How about Thursday?"

"Okay," Sara said, nodding. "You might have to help me carry Sheridan."

"That's fine."

"I saw Renee," Sara said, nodding across the street toward the gallery. "Said she stopped by the cottage for some of your beautiful new pottery and a cup of lukewarm java."

Eden smiled uneasily. Her friends were forever teasing her about her last-second preparations for their weekly get-together over break-fast. "You just wait. Next time you two come to my place, the cof-fee'll be hot and the table ready for a photographer from *Bon Appetit*."

"Sure, sure." Sara straightened a stack on her wide desk. "Renee seemed unsettled. Did you two argue?"

"Nah. She wanted me to go to Seattle with her, but I wasn't up for it."

"Why?"

"I have a date to go hiking with you Thursday," Eden said, picking up her book and backpack. "I can't leave now."

"Eden—"

"See you Thursday," she interrupted. "Give Sheridan a kiss from me!"

Nick dumped his bag to the floor of the cabin, and a puff of dust shot up from either side. Jared grunted and tried the overhead light, an ancient wrought-iron configuration with eight bare bulbs in a circle. Three lit up.

"This place is a pit," Nicolaus announced.

"You're right," Jared said. "Want to stay someplace else?"

"Nah. Let's look around." He went over to the far wall and pulled aside old curtains with a western design. "Look, Dad! You can see the river from here."

Jared joined him at the window and stared out at the shining ribbon that cut the forest with a serpentine path. The June waters looked high and fast—probably still gathering snowmelt runoff, he mused.

"Can I go down there?"

"No!" Jared said, more harshly than he intended. "No, Nick. Not without me. Never without me. Got it?"

"Yeah," Nicolaus said, giving him a puzzled look. "Whatever." He turned toward the nearest stack of junk. "Hey, look at this." He held up an old army knife.

"Let me see that," Jared said. He took it and examined it. "Probably World War I." He handed it back to his son.

"Can I keep it?"

"Sure. Just be careful."

"Cool!" The boy turned to the stacks again, as if ready to dig for more treasure.

"Hold on. Let's go find our beds and unload the car. Then we can clean out enough stuff from the kitchen counters and hallways to make it livable. We have our work cut out for us."

"Aw, Dad. I want to go outside!"

Jared considered his son for a moment. The truth was, he wanted to be outside in the fresh, clean air rather than in the dank cabin himself. Nick gave him a pleading look. "All right. Help me get our luggage inside; then you can go explore outside. As long as you keep the cabin in sight and don't go down to the river without me."

"All right." He bounded out the door, as excited as a kid at camp.

Jared looked around again. It was no wonder the real estate agent didn't want to do this herself. It would take weeks to get the place in shape. He smiled and found himself warming to the challenge. *You must really need a break, Conway. This is the saddest excuse for a vacation I've ever heard of.*

On Thursday, Eden groaned when her alarm went off at five. She could hear the coffee brewing in the kitchen, thanks to her new pot with a timer, a birthday gift from Renee. The aroma eased the shock of such an early awakening. Rubbing her eyes, she swung her legs out from under the down comforter and let her toes brush the cool wooden floors. She slipped into her lambskin moccasins as she reached for her terry robe. Padding out to the kitchen, she wearily filled a mug, then as was her custom, walked to the door to survey the lake. Even in the dark, the stillness of the beach spoke to her. Over the years she had come to read the lake like a dear old friend, and it treated her as such, allowing her to bare her soul to the empty waters. Rain was likely today, she surmised from its quietude, but probably not until later.

She turned to hurriedly throw some bread under the broiler, dress, and fill her canteen with water. If she was late for their hike, Sara would not be happy. After all, it had been some time since the woman had gotten up at this hour, other than to feed the baby, and odds were she'd give up altogether if she didn't have Eden there to encourage her. Eden yawned as she laced her hiking boots. She still hadn't caught up on her sleep since the morning she'd awakened early to sculpt the troubled woman.

The scent of browning bread drew her to the kitchen. After spreading the toasted slices with butter, she wrapped them in a cloth napkin and headed to her truck. She paused on the porch, staring at the figure that still startled her, as if it were a living presence. She bent to unwrap the plastic around it, and noticing an odd hump in the figure's neck, licked her fingers and reworked it. Eden sat back, nodding in pleasure at the revised curve. Suddenly she remembered what she was supposed to be doing and checked her watch. She had ten minutes to get to town. Sara would be waiting.

She ran to the truck, revved the engine, and quickly turned the rig around, the balding tires searching for traction. She might save a minute or two if she took the back roads to town. She turned left, rounded the corner, and approached the bridge. The sun was coming up, and she was just about to turn out her headlights and enjoy the peaked, ethereal pinks and golds of sunrise when she thought she saw someone in the center of the structure. Her hand eased off the light knob; she leaned forward, squinted, and slowed the truck.

He stood in the very center of the bridge, hands gripping the rail, staring down in perfect stillness as if in another world. She didn't know him. Decked out in jogging gear, he didn't look up. But she could tell, even with just a quick glance, that he wasn't a local. She wondered if she should stop and ask if there was anything wrong. But he was clearly all right. Simply out for an early morning jog, just as she was setting out for an early morning hike. Still, there was something about him, something about his stance, that made her wonder what he saw, what he was looking for...

She shook her head. She was just being nosy.

And Sara was waiting.

"That right-wing blow-hard fired me, Anna," Rick said from the kitchen doorway as she boiled a milk bottle for the baby.

She turned from the stove, aghast. "No, Rick. Not another one."

"It wasn't my fault!" he defended, going to the fridge to peer inside, then shut it in frustration. "I went outside for a smoke on my break, and the guy said I stole the cigarettes."

"Did you?"

"Of course not!"

"Did you tell him that?"

"Do you think I'm a total idiot? I told him he'd been smokin' somethin' a whole lot stronger if he thought I had stolen those cigs."

"Ah. Good one. What, Rick? Did you want to get fired?"

"What's that supposed to mean?" He leaned toward her menacingly as he asked the question. Jared was wailing from their bedroom—hungry, she supposed. Anna turned away from Rick and went to the stove, reaching for the hot pan, her mind on how they were going to make ends meet. It would be up to her, no doubt. Again. She cried out as the heat seared her palm.

Rick was right beside her. "Oh, man. C'mon, over to the sink." He led her across the cheap, decaying linoleum to the chipped porcelain bowl and turned on the water, which came out in airy spurts. "Here, keep it under there. I'll get you some ice from the freezer." He returned a second later.

"The baby," she said, still wincing over the red-hot pain on her palm.

"Don't worry about it, sweetheart. His daddy will go feed him. You take care of yourself."

As he hurried away, Anna wondered about how he could be so mean one second and so kind the next.

CHAPTER THREE

On the first day of July, Eden was preparing to surprise her friends with a complete breakfast laid out for them when they came to her cabin for coffee. Freshly baked scones and homemade huckleberry jam awaited on a table completely set—even with a tablecloth—while a heavenly asparagus and Swiss cheese omelet kept warm in the oven. Eden, pleased with how it all looked, was eager for Sara and Renee to arrive.

It was a perfect summer morning, and Eden briefly held out some hope that the Fourth of July might actually be a nice day. Traditionally it was one of the worst in the valley, often rainy and cold. At eight o'clock it was already sixty-five degrees, boding well for a bone-warming day on the deck. Eden smiled when she heard Renee's car on the drive and went out to meet her friends. But the two women barely acknowledged her, so intent was their discussion about the man they had seen on the bridge half a mile down the road.

Eden's heart did an odd flip at their mention of him. She had seen the man several times as he ran, and somehow she had begun to think of him over the last week as her own little secret, allowing herself to fantasize about meeting him but not letting her dreams get out of hand. It was something to do as she sculpted.

"So, who's the handsome new neighbor, Eden?" Renee asked.

She wrapped a thin arm around Eden's shoulders, and Eden suddenly felt fat and big beside her. One look at Renee and the jogger would do flips. Renee had perfect skin and huge blue eyes laced with lashes that could have belonged to a doe. Her long nose and face were aristocratic, perfect for her long, lithe body.

"I don't know," she said with a careless shrug, pulling away too quickly.

"So you've seen him too," Renee said. She crossed her arms. Even her nails were perfectly manicured.

Eden checked herself. What was wrong with her? Why the sudden competition? She sighed. Whatever was to be, would be. She wasn't interested in romantic entanglements anyway. "He showed up a couple of weeks ago, about the time you left for Seattle. I've seen him out running several times but most often on the bridge. He stands there and stares and stares at the water."

"He didn't even look up when we passed him," Sara said, opening the squeaky screen door.

"It was like he was in a trance," Renee added.

"Maybe he was just thinking," Eden said. She paused at the awkward note of defensiveness in her voice.

Renee shot her an odd look, then went in the house behind Sara.

"What's that heavenly smell?" Sara asked as she headed directly to the oven.

"Scones!" Renee said, lifting the cloth over the bowl. "And look at your table! So beautiful!"

Sara opened the oven door. "You cooked! Renee, she's got an omelet in here!"

"No," her friend responded, feigning shock to tease their friend.

Eden ignored their playful jibes. "Coffee?" she offered. "You haven't told me about Seattle yet, Renee. Meet any eligible bachelors this time?"

Renee pursed her lips and carefully studied Eden's face. "You're intrigued with the man on the bridge too. You're telling me to back off."

Eden made a sound in derision. "I don't know what you're talking about."

"Yes, you do. I just can't believe it. I thought you were never going to chance it again."

"Renee…" Sara warned.

"How could she have ignored him? I'm glad you're even *thinking* about the guy." Renee smiled like a Cheshire cat. "I'm happy to back off."

"Should I get the omelet?" Sara whispered. Eden nodded. She had carefully orchestrated the entire morning, and now Renee had taken the conductor's stick. There was no use fighting it; she might as well play out the whole concerto.

Renee sat back in the wicker chair, placing the cloth napkin on her lap as she delicately crossed her slim legs and studied Eden. "So?"

"So?"

"How are you going to meet him?"

"I don't know," Eden said. The thought of it made her suddenly want to run away.

Sara arrived with the omelet and sat down across from Renee, leaving Eden in the middle as usual. The two were like the opposite sides of a quarter, with Eden the copper in between. "I'll say grace,"

Eden said quietly, and after a brief blessing they passed the food in silence.

"You could go jogging yourself," Sara suggested. With the boost from Eden, she had gotten back into hiking five miles almost every morning, her baby in a carrier on her back.

"I'm more of a swimmer."

"Become a new running enthusiast," Renee directed.

"You're one to talk."

"Hey, if that man was on my bridge, I'd get into shape. You're already in shape."

"I don't know. I tend to think if it's supposed to happen, it will."

"How?" Renee asked, fork poised before her, full of fluffy omelet. "You'll be backing out your driveway and accidentally hit him? You said yourself that he's pretty absorbed on the bridge. And when he's running, it's hard to stop him for directions. Especially since you *live* here."

"I'll find a way," Eden defended. "Something will come up."

"I hope so," Renee said with concern on her face. "I swear, girl, you've become a recluse."

"I have not." She looked to Sara for affirmation.

"Sorry. She's right," her friend said to her unspoken question.

"You have!" Renee continued, drawing Eden's gaze. "I threw that singles' party at the gallery last year, and what did she do?" Eden glanced at Sara, who was no help, since as a happily married woman, she had not been invited. "She sat in the corner, pretending to be overly interested in the work of a ceramist from Missoula."

"Not all night."

"Most of it. So, the question remains. If you go out walking with Sara and bump into him, what will you say?"

" 'Hey there, Mr. Fabulous, you from 'round these parts?' "

Both of her friends cracked up. "Perfect," Sara said. She turned toward Renee. "She'll come up with something. I promise."

"Okay. But remember, I'll hold you accountable for getting her to say something. No more hermithood for this girl. We won't allow it."

Eden shook her head. "Just what I need. A couple of conspirators for friends." She took a sip of coffee. "He's probably just one of the summer people." A part of her hoped it was true. It would get her off the hook and kill her unrealistic dreams.

"It's early yet for summer people," Sara said.

"He's already been here a couple weeks," Renee added. "You'll know next week. Most of 'em leave after two. If he's still around, maybe he's a new resident."

"Maybe," Eden said slowly.

With a flourish, Jared placed a heavily loaded plate on the table in front of his son. Fat French toast triangles were spread out in an arc and sprinkled with powdered sugar. A generous slice of ham accompanied it.

"No thanks," Nicolaus said glumly. "I think I'll just go have cereal with Michael."

Jared frowned and sat down across the table from him. "No, Nick. I'd like you to eat with me today."

"Why today?" his eight-year-old challenged. "The last couple of weeks, you've been happy to leave me next door while you work or run."

"I thought you liked going to the Sundquists'."

"I do. That's why I want to go again today."

"I don't think they want to feed you every day. Listen, Nick, I know I've been busy with the cabin, but I'm making headway."

"Outside, but look at this place." Together they gazed around the log cabin, still crammed with stacks of newspapers and magazines and boxes. It was a fine, sturdy home of huge logs and soaring ceilings, with two small bedrooms in back. The chinking needed to be redone, Julie Vose had told him, but the rest of the structure was sound.

"I sold that old rusted tractor yesterday to some high-class decorator. Said she wanted it for the landscape design of a new log home up near the ski resort in Whitefish."

"I liked that thing. We should've kept it." Reluctantly the boy cut a piece of French toast and put it into his mouth. "Michael and I played on it," he said, still chewing.

"Don't talk with your mouth full." Jared clamped his lips shut. The boy was finally talking to him, and he used the moment to reprimand him. *Good parenting technique, Jared,* he derided himself. "How 'bout I bail on my running and the cabin today, and we go get that fishing gear?"

"You mean it?" the boy said, visibly brightening.

"Yeah. I've seen you and Mike out on their dock. You're getting a good hand with that fly rod. You deserve one of your own."

"Caught a rainbow yesterday that was eighteen inches," the boy boasted. Jared had begun to allow him to fish from the dock as long as he wore a life vest.

"Why didn't you bring it home for dinner?"

"I told you, Dad. It's catch and release here."

"Oh yeah." Jared had remembered. It just felt good to be having a conversation with his son. "When I was in Alaska that one time, I caught one over two feet long."

"No way."

"Way."

"Did you see any bears?"

"One, but he was far away. More elk and moose."

"Michael was going to show me a beaver's dam today. Can I still go with him?"

"After we go to town, I suppose."

"Can we go to Two River Gear? Michael says their stuff is awesome."

"Wherever you want. And when you go looking for that dam, I want you to wear your life vest."

"Aw, Dad. Michael doesn't have to wear one. We're going to be walking, not—"

"Wear it or don't go."

The boy sighed heavily. After a moment he said, "Dad?"

"Yeah?"

"How much longer are we gonna be here?"

"I don't know," Jared said, pausing over his French toast. "Your mom's been calling. She wants to see you this summer too. I just didn't anticipate how much work was involved in cleaning this place up. When the real estate agent said there was too much for her to do, she wasn't kidding."

"I could spend all summer here."

Jared smiled. The place had caught him by surprise too. After detoxing from his frantic eighty-hour workweeks, he had settled in to the quiet pace of the Swan River and the valley. He relished the peace now, the easing winds on the water, a place to run in the open air, away from smog. He'd even gotten the office to stop calling—for the most part—reclaiming the two years' vacation he had not taken and leaving the business in Don's hands. The only commodity Jared was interested in this month was his son.

"You don't miss TV?"

"Michael's family has a dish."

Jared laughed under his breath. No wonder Nick was over there all the time. He had seen his son out with the neighbor boy enough, though, not to be concerned with how much television he was watching. And the Sundquists were good people. Still, here it was the first of July already, and it was obvious that he hadn't spent enough time with Nick to make a difference in their relationship. He wanted to be closer to his son, connected. And this was the week to do it, he decided. They had spent three weeks getting used to living with each other again; now it was time to get to know each other, too.

A week later, they had the fishing vests, rods, line, flies, boots, and Nick had even gotten waders. As they put into the river, Jared smiled. It was a perfect day for a father-son outing. A pristine mountain morning to teach his child how to fish. If Nick thought fishing from the dock was fun, he was in for an exciting revelation; fishing from a boat was much more interesting. The landscape was ever changing, the opportunity to find a hiding trout ever present.

The Sundquists had dropped them off at Blair's Landing and promised to leave their car at the bridge by Porcupine Creek, about seven miles distant. Jared had estimated it would take them about three hours to reach it, depending upon how often they stopped. It was beautiful, isolated country. Lush, grassy banks gave way to rounded, forested hills beyond. High above towered blue mountain peaks. A soft breeze rustled through the leaves of cotton-wood and aspen near the water, and the swiftly rising sun glistened on the river.

Jared smiled in appreciation, then dipped the oars in again as he directed Nicolaus on technique. "Right there, Nick. Over by the bank." He nodded toward the river's edge, undercut by the high water. "They'll like the dark there." He had learned a few things from his guide in Alaska three summers back. He hoped he remembered enough to be a good teacher to his son.

The boat rocked as Nick cast and moved to the edge in one motion, making Jared's heart leap. "*Careful, Nick!* Careful," he repeated, this time more softly. The boy could be so oblivious to the dangers of the river that it made Jared angry. The last thing they needed was to roll into the river. Both had life vests on, but still. He warily eyed his son's waders. Nick had insisted on wearing them, and Jared intended to stop once in a while and fish from the shore with him, so he had grudgingly given in.

"There you go. Back and forth, back and forth," he coached. He winced and ducked as the fly came perilously close to his eye. "Careful!" He sighed. It wasn't going to be easy, managing the boat and his eight-year-old at the same time. Maybe around the next bend they would pull up and get the hang of their new gear from shore. He put his shoulders to the oars, pulling against the current that was urging them toward a boulder, and guided them safely around it. The river curved and opened up again. They startled a mallard, and he took off with a deep-throated *guh-guh-guh* in complaint. Jared took a deep, steadying breath, reminding himself to enjoy this, to not lose the moment because of his own fears. The river smelled of pitch and pine and pollen, of roots and reeds and rocks.

"Dad! There's somebody else fishing!" The boy waved, as excited as if he were seeing another person for the first time in a year.

"Yeah. Pay attention to what you're doing. That's it. How 'bout over by those logs? Yes. They love anyplace they can feel safer. The closer you can get to it, the better. But try not to get caught up. Ease it out. A little farther this time. That's it. A little closer."

The water was moving swiftly. Jared pulled steadily against it, wanting to give his son a little more time near the logs.

"Oh! Oh no! I'm caught!" Nicolaus cried. He pulled against it, bending his rod into a fierce arc.

"Hold on, Nick. I'll row back! Pull gently. Not so hard. Try to get the fly dislodged." Jared dug against the current, gradually reaching the snag that had captured Nick's line. For the first time he spotted a boulder holding the logjam in place and the whirlpool current just beyond it.

"I can see it!" The boy slid to the opposite side of the boat, reaching for the log.

"Whoa!" Jared shouted, counterbalancing his son's sudden move. "Hold on. *No!* No, Nick!" In horror, Jared watched as his son suddenly stood and reached out for the fly. He did reach it—right before he fell in. Jared leaned forward, trying to grab him, but missed. One oar slipped out of its rounder and drifted away, but Jared was staring at his son, who came up sputtering, the life vest doing its job, the fly in his hand. "Got it!" he cried.

Jared laughed in relief and put a hand under the shoulder of the boy's life vest. "Come on. Let's get you back in." They were drifting away from the logs, closer to the boulder, but his attention was on his child. His smile faded. Nick was getting heavier and more difficult to hold. "Grab my hand, Nick," he said urgently.

The boy frowned, sinking up to his chin. "Dad…"

"Nick, grab my hand!" Jared ground out, leaning precariously over the edge in order to get a better grip on his son to haul him aboard. How could he be getting heavier? Sinking? Then it dawned on him—the waders! They were like a parachute in the wind. "Nick, your waders! Can you get them off?" The boat nosed into a dip caused by the boulder's presence and then paused as if caught in an eddy.

Nicolaus dipped to his eyebrows, but then came up again, his legs drifting with the river's current, under the boat. His small, white hands clung to the metal edge of the boat.

"The waders, Nick! Release the waders! I can't hold on much longer!" He gritted his teeth against the strain, but still the boy grew heavier. Madly he looked about, his eyes landing on the woman on shore. She had dropped her pole, obviously aware that they were in trouble.

"I can't pull him in!" Panic engulfed him, paralyzed him. He heard her dive in but was not watching. Instead he saw his son go under again, the life vest wrenching away from Jared's hand. "No!" he cried. *"No!"* Nick disappeared under the boat, drifting with the current.

Panting in fear and frustration, Jared shifted to the other side of the boat. The rocking motion edged them out of the boulder's eddy.

The fisherwoman reached them with strong strokes, dove under, and pulled the boy to the surface. She eyed the beach, twenty feet distant, and then the child, making a quick decision. "Here. I've got him. Secure yourself," she directed Jared, "and grab both sides of the vest. I'm going to take those waders off you, kid. Grab hold of the boat and help your dad keep you in place."

She took a deep breath and went under, prying the rubber pants off the child as she leveraged herself against the boat. The waders peeled off easily, and Jared pulled him up and into his arms.

The woman surfaced and swam toward them. "Toss me a line," she said.

Numbly, Jared threw her a rope, while still holding on to Nick. She swam toward the beach, touched bottom, and hauled them inward.

As soon as they were safely ashore, Jared turned Nick toward him, shaking him. "Nick, I told you to not lean over the side! You totally ignored what I said!" Enraged in his terror, he shook him again.

"Hey!" the woman yelled. "Knock it off."

"Stay out of it," Jared growled. He turned back to Nicolaus. "You could have died! I could have lost you! I could have lost you!" The tears came then, unbidden. "I could have lost you," he wept, pulling the child to his chest and sinking to the beach. "I'm sorry," Jared groaned, shaking his head, caressing Nick's face, holding him tight. "I'm so sorry," he said to his son. "I should have been more careful. I should have thought it through."

Finally he looked at the woman, his face ashen. "Thank you. Thank you. And I'm sorry for yelling at you. I was so scared—"

She shook her head, panting, hands on knees, breaking their intense gaze. "Didn't do anything that anyone else wouldn't have done." She stood and threw back her shoulder-length brown hair. "That boy ought not be in waders. They're deathtraps."

"I can see that. I thought about it…wondered about it…" Jared felt disoriented, faint, like the time he'd had the flu and spiked a temperature of a hundred and four. He stared on down the river, watching the landscape tilt one way and then the other.

"Dad! You can let go now. You're hurting me. Oh, man. I lost my pole."

"Good we didn't lose you," the woman said.

Jared released him but still stroked his face, his shoulders, wanting to make sure he was whole, as fine as he claimed to be. The fisherwoman set off down the beach to retrieve their oar from some brush on the bank. By the time she returned, the dizziness had abated. Nick stood on the beach, tossing rocks into the water as if nothing had happened at all.

The woman coughed. "I'd better get home and get some dry clothes on. I assume you have a way to your own dry clothes."

Jared nodded, wondering what he could do for this woman to repay her. What an idiot she must have thought he was, putting himself and his child in danger like that. "Listen, the least I could do would be to have your clothes cleaned—"

She looked down at her soaked jeans and blouse, and then they both laughed uneasily, happy to break the tense moment.

"All right, then buy you a new outfit," he said.

"No. That's all right. Jeans and a shirt will do just fine in the wash. I'll dry out."

"Will you be all right?"

"Fine, fine. Better get that boy home to his mother. And watch yourselves," she added.

"Nick's mom is in New York. It's just me and him this summer," he said. "I'm Jared Conway. This is my son, Nicolaus." The boy looked just like his father. Jared reached out a large hand. "And I really am sorry."

She took it, smiling as the warmth of his big palm enveloped her cold one. "Eden Powell. And don't mention it. As I said, anyone would have done the same."

"You live nearby?"

"No, on the lake. North end. But my car's here. The fish weren't biting anyway; I may as well head back and get into dry clothes."

"We're staying on the river near the north end of the lake," he offered. "In my Uncle Rudy's old cabin."

"Ahh," she said. "I knew Rudy Conway. He was a good man." She paused a moment, then said, "You weren't at the memorial service, were you?"

"We weren't that close. Didn't know Uncle Rudy had died until a lawyer called and gave me the news. He left me the cabin. Guess there wasn't anyone else."

"I see. Nice gift. A bit crowded in there, but it could be great if you got out from under all the garbage. He was a pack rat, your uncle."

"Yes. I'm beginning to see a little of its potential. I have one wall in one bedroom cleared out, plus most of the grounds."

"That's makin' some progress," she said appreciatively. She turned away. "I hope the rest of your fishing is in dry duds, Nick," she tossed over her shoulder. Jared watched as she walked back to her fishing gear.

"Thanks, Miss Powell."

Jared watched as she moved through the brush and trees toward an old red truck, set her gear in the back, and then climbed into the cab. She gave them a shy smile and waved a little, then turned around and drove off down a poorly kept dirt road.

He turned back to his son. "Thank God Miss Powell was there," he said. "Come here," he motioned, opening his arms. He pulled the reluctant child close. "I don't ever want to come that close to losing you again, Nick. Never again."

When Anna's hand became infected, she was forced to go to the hospital. She could tell Rick felt responsible—he paced around, holding their child in his arms, as they waited for an emergency-room doctor to take a look. It had been a week since the burn had occurred, and it was getting worse instead of better.

"Miss? The doctor will see you now," a nurse said, waiting expectantly by the door. Anna rose obediently, and Rick followed behind, carrying their son.

"You the husband?" the nurse asked. She looked up at Rick suspiciously. Many looked at him that way since he'd grown his beard and hair long.

"No, I—"

"Then you'll have to wait outside. She'll be out shortly." Swiftly she closed the door in his face. A thump sounded behind them, betraying Rick's anger. The nurse glanced at Anna, but Anna carefully looked away.

After reviewing her chart, the doctor said, "You're running a slight temp." He unwrapped the bandage on her hand, a kerchief she had wound around it. "Nothing sterile at home?" he asked gently.

"I boiled it. Tried to get it super clean before I put it on."

He carefully prodded and moved her hand to see the burn from different angles.

"I work as a maid. It gets wet a lot."

"I see. Can't have that any longer. You need to keep it dry. You really shouldn't use it. You're opening it up every time you do."

"I gotta use it," she told him. "I have a baby at home and a full-time job. It's not like I can sit back and watch TV."

"Shall I call social services?" he asked kindly. "They can help, you know."

"No, no. We're okay. If you could just give me some medicine, I'm sure it will get better soon."

"All right," the doctor said with a sigh. "I'll send you home with some samples, but you need to try and not use your hand."

As the doctor left, Rick snuck in, his arms full with the baby in the crook of one elbow, a vase of flowers in the other.

"Rick, we can't afford those!"

"Shush. You deserve them."

Overwhelmed, she smiled and examined each blossom, each petal. Never had she received flowers, not even the day she'd had Jared. "Thanks, Rick."

"You're welcome, sweetheart," he said, kissing her tenderly on the temple. "What did the doctor say?"

He came in then again, looking from Rick to Anna. "Take care of that hand now." He stared hard at Rick. "She needs to try and not use it."

"Gotcha," Rick said with a duck of his head. "I'll take care of her."

They were on their way home before Anna wondered how Rick had paid for the flowers. Her heart sank. He had to have stolen them. From another room or the front desk, somewhere. He hadn't had a penny to his name in weeks. "Did you steal these flowers, Rick?" she asked softly. "You took them, didn't you?"

CHAPTER FOUR

Jared finished tying the ancient mattress to the top of his BMW and threw the remaining rope through the passenger-side window. "Come on, Nick!" he called. His boy was up in a tree with their neighbor Michael and scrambled down quickly.

"Where're we going?" he asked.

"The dump. I'm getting two new mattresses today." He was sick to death of the sagging, lumpy old thing he slept on. Nick hadn't complained, but Jared had gone ahead and ordered a new one for his room, too, for good measure.

"Cool," the boy said, at an age when other people's junk could be his treasure.

"We're not staying around for long," Jared warned.

"Okay. Five minutes?"

"Five minutes," Jared said with a smile. He remembered his summers in Vermont, and how he and his cousins had loved to do the exact same thing. When they pulled into the dump, two miles down the road, an old man in a battered Ford truck was pulling out. Seeing the mattress on top of Jared's luxury sedan made the old man laugh out loud and shake his head. Jared could imagine how it looked. Definitely like out-of-towners.

"Hey, look over there!" Nick exclaimed. At a corner Dumpster was a brown bear, on his hind legs, looking from them to his prospective meal inside.

"Oh! Don't get out of the car, Nick!" He honked the horn and the bear got down on all fours, wagged his head at them as if shaking it in disgust and then ran off.

Nicolaus hooted in pleasure, and Jared laughed with him. "Don't see that very often at Buckley, do you?"

"Nope! That was cool! Wait until I tell Michael!"

"Here, help me get this off the car," Jared said, untying the mattress. The boy wasn't that much help, but Jared enjoyed doing anything with him, eager to share everything—the day after almost losing him—to remind himself that Nick really was all right. They heaved and grunted and finally hauled the old thing over to the dumpster, panting from the exertion. Jared cast a wary eye to the forest, but the bear was apparently gone for good.

"Look at that old chair," Nick said, pointing toward a decrepit rocker with springs sticking out.

"Uh-huh," Jared said, worried that his son would want to bring it home.

"And there's an old stove!"

"Yes. Let's get on back, okay?"

"All right," the boy said glumly. "Last week Michael found an old surfboard here!"

"A surfboard? Now there's a usable object in northwest Montana."

"He's going to get a friend to tow him behind a boat on the lake."

"Sounds like fun. That was a lucky find, I guess."

"Yeah. It has a big hole in it, but it's all right." Jared slipped his hand around the boy's narrow neck, appreciating the time they had together. Their brief holidays as a family were always too short; already they had been together five days longer than at any other time since Nick had gone to Buckley. They were connecting here in a new way, *bonding* as the psychologists would say. Their close call yesterday had even brought them closer. And it felt good.

They got in his car and headed down the road, which ran alongside the river in places. There was a tie to his mother here, in this mountain country, that Jared hadn't anticipated. He had remembered that she'd died here, of course. He just had never thought about her living here, loving it here. It made what little he knew of her come alive, giving him a sense of history, a sense of foundation in Rudy's old place. And it made it all the more important to have his son with him there.

Eden dived into the cold, clear waters of the lake, immediately heading south, as she did every morning of the summer. It was about a half-mile of swimming, and it left her ready for her day as nothing else could. Using a breaststroke, she made her way to the point—her quarter-mile check—and crawled out onto a big, sloping, black granite boulder that edged into the lake. It was always sun warm, and she liked to lay upon it for a few moments each morning, drawing the heat into her body before returning to the chilling waters to get back to her dock.

Rarely were there people about at that hour, most choosing to wait until midmorning or after lunch to begin their lake activities. So she had the place to herself and could sunbathe in privacy. On her stomach, chin on her hands, she stared down the lake to the Swan Peaks—gray-lavender, towering mountains that held on to

great patches of snow until late July—thinking about the man and
boy she had encountered the day before. Few people entered her
mind and stayed there. She couldn't get Jared and Nick out of it.

What if she hadn't been able to grab Nick? What would have
happened to them? Would Jared have gone in the water to reach
him? Drowning people often took others down with them. Would
Nick have panicked, climbed atop Jared to try to save himself,
killing them both? Would Jared have been able to pull the waders off
of Nick? She breathed another prayer of thanks that God had spared
the boy, then determined not to think about it for one more minute.

She looked around. The lake was awakening for the summer,
visitors arriving en masse. She was willing to share her special part of
the world for a couple of months, almost looked forward to the fren-
zied activity through July and August, because it always made her so
glad when the peace of autumn rolled around. The valley was a
unique, sacred place. She hoped Jared and Nick appreciated it too.

She eased back into the water and headed for home.

They were almost back to the cabin when Nick thought of it. "We
should get Miss Powell some flowers," he said. "You know, as thanks
for helping us out yesterday."

Jared nodded. "That would be really nice, Nick. Let's do it." He
pulled out his cell phone and handed it to his son. "Call information. Ask for a florist in Bigfork."

"Nah," Nicolaus said. "Look!" He gestured to the side of the
road, toward a field of daisies at the end of their growth season. "And
we have fireweed and bluebells at home, around where the old tractor was."

Jared smiled and nodded. He wondered if Michael had taught his son the names of the local flora. "Right. Who needs a florist?"

When they got home, Nicolaus was immediately out the door, intent upon his mission of finding flowers for their river benefactor. Not that Jared wasn't a willing participant. It was just that he didn't want to remember Nick going under, disappearing... He shuddered. He couldn't stand the thought of losing Nick. Not to the river. Not anywhere.

His first thought was to run the flowers by later that day, but Nick thought it would be more fun to leave them on her porch for her to find when she awakened in the morning—a "surprise," he called it. When they had each gathered a huge fistful and returned indoors, it was his son who found the urn to put them in. It needed a good polish, but it had a certain charm amidst the tarnish. It was as if the wildflowers fit better in something old, simple, imperfect.

They left the cabin at first light the following morning, Nick still rubbing the sleep from his eyes, and drove up the hill and over the new bridge to the road that led to Eden's side of the lake. Jared had a pretty good idea which house was hers, and he was right. The airy cottage was within view of the bridge. POWELL was on the mailbox in neat, hand-painted lettering. They set the urn on the open back porch, the one that faced the lake, and Jared covered Nick's mouth when he giggled, stifling his own laughter as he did so. How long had it been since they had done something so fun together? The fishing expedition two days before had started out as fun but had quickly turned to disaster. Doing something nice for another, really working at it, gave him a warm feeling in his gut; it was better than the relief of ordering two dozen roses for Patricia on her birthday or Mother's Day or their anniversary...

Patricia. The comparison made him think of her call the night before. She hadn't even asked how he was, only wondered "where on earth they had disappeared to," then asked when he intended to "bring my son home."

He would find a way to actually voice his thanks to Eden later. For now the flowers were enough. He frowned slightly as they climbed back in his BMW, still idling on the gravel road beyond the cottage. What if Eden had a boyfriend? Someone else she would credit for the flowers? He wanted her to know they were from them. He sighed and turned the car around, back toward the river, almost ready to let it happen as it may, when he stopped.

Jared pulled out his wallet and a business card and quickly wrote on the back:

> *Thanks for fishing the two*
> *of us out of the river wild.*
> *—Nick and Jared*

He circled his cell phone number on the front and handed it over to Nick. "Here, go put that in the flowers."

"Okay," the boy agreed. He eagerly ran off to do as his father bid. They were making some progress as father and son, Jared thought, irritatingly slow but assuredly forward.

Eden awakened that morning and yawned heartily. It had been a fit-ful night of sleep, her thoughts interrupted by images of drowning children and mysterious fishermen. Jared Conway was trouble; she could sense it. God was probably telling her to steer clear. She slipped out from under her down comforter, pulled on a thick terry-cloth robe, and padded out to the kitchen across wide-planked wooden floors. Her cottage, built in the '40s, was in the shape of a square, its wraparound porch screened on the north to protect occupants from mosquitoes and other unpleasant flying creatures.

The structure had been angled to catch the best views down the lake, past tiny islands and heavily forested, curving banks to the Swan peaks at the far end. Eden had fallen in love with it at first sight, and over the years had refurbished it to make it contemporary, to make it hers.

The spare bedroom that she used as a ramshackle office led into a large, open family room, which bordered a tiny galley kitchen, and next to that was her own bedroom and bathroom. She had redone the kitchen counters in stainless steel, the sink in concrete the color of the pine trees outside her door. The walls were heavily plastered and painted a soft ivory, contrasting with the deep hues of the natural wood all about her. In the center was a stone fireplace that opened into the family room on one side and her bedroom on the other. From her bedroom she could climb a narrow flight of stairs to the attic, a broad, open room—aside from the chimney which rose from the center and up through the roof—which she used as her studio when it was too cold to be on the porch.

She loved her little house. The walls featured simple, whimsical watercolors and warm, lush oil paintings depicting various scenes from around her beloved Montana, all done by acquaintances far and wide. In the stairwell were pictures of her family and dearest friends, matted with thick borders and framed with simple silver. She had had them all reprinted as sepiatones, creating a monochromatic, antique feel.

She went first to the coffee maker, pressing the button to start the brew she had set up the night before when she hadn't been able to sleep and found herself pacing. She hadn't set the timer as she usually did, hoping she would sleep in. Hearing the comforting sounds of the water dripping, Eden went to the cupboard and pulled out the heel of her last loaf of bread. Perhaps she would bake a new batch if the day was warm enough for dough to rise properly. After placing the slice under the broiler of the old stove she had rescued from her great-grandparents' cabin, she padded toward the wood-framed floor-to-ceiling glass door. She had redone all the windows to capitalize on the breathtaking views all about her—from lush pines to the gray lake, wind rushing northward as it often did on mornings that evolved into perfect afternoons.

Eden smiled at the whitecaps on the tiny waves that crossed the narrow lake. It promised to be a good day for bread baking. Her eyes ran the length of the lake, and she was turning to go back to check on her toast when her eyes found the tarnished silver urn, tightly filled with wildflowers. She let out a small gasp and quickly looked around, wondering who had left such a beautiful gift on her porch. There was no one about. Tucking her robe more tightly around her neck, she opened the door and stepped out into the cool morning air. She picked up the urn and brought it inside, placing it on her kitchen table.

Her eyes went back to it again and again as she poured her coffee and buttered her toast. Renee? No, she would have polished the antique urn. Sara? No, she was too busy with her family to dash out just to leave flowers. It was then she saw the small card, tucked in the center. She pulled it out, one hand to her mouth. *Jared Conway.* He had a nice logo on his card, good graphic design. *He's a commodities broker.* She turned it over and read the words, smiling.

Eden cupped her chin and stared at the beautiful mix of fireweed, bluebells, and tiny white daisies. It had been a long, long time since anyone had given her flowers. She frowned suddenly. Who knew if he was even someone she wanted to know? He seemed nice enough, yes, but maybe he wasn't even available—after all, "it's just the two of us" could mean several different things. But his tone had said divorce.

Her heart told her he was risky, to turn away. She sighed. She was leaping to all sorts of conclusions, which wasn't like her. Eden turned away from the flowers. She needed to get her head clear. She would go for a quick swim and then walk to her praying spot, to spend some time trying to understand what God had to tell her. If she was fortunate enough to be able to concentrate on the Lord at all.

Two hours later, Nicolaus flew out the door toward Michael's house and Jared again turned toward the wall of papers and boxes that lined the living room area of the cabin. The old house was made of thick logs, solid and straight. A living room with vaulted ceilings eased into a small kitchen on one side. On the far wall a huge fireplace made of river rock rose to the gently sloped roof. Beyond it, on either side, doors led to the two bedrooms, and between them, practically stuck on the outside, was a bathroom. It looked as if Rudy had added it on sometime in the '60s.

Jared had been on the river with Nick for almost three weeks, and the work was painfully slow now that he was inside. Outside it had been physical work, with big results as huge pieces were sold or given away. Inside his work was reduced to tedious, menial sorting in the dim light. After he tossed another ancient newspaper to his "dump" pile and sneezed, he blew his nose and looked at the old windows. They needed to be refinished, maybe even replaced. But that would be up to the new owners. He was going to empty this place out, hire a cleaning lady, and invite Ms. Vose back for a new assessment. Nick and he would leave with happy memories and go back to their lives in New York.

He stared at the next paper in the stack, a brief note in a woman's handwriting, not reading the words. He was envisioning leaving this place, and the feeling made him melancholy. He looked up again at the windows and then rose, stretching out his arms to measure them. Only five feet wide, they could be replaced with bigger windows—longer windows, allowing in more light. He turned and stared at the kitchen. It could be refurbished, expanded, to make it more usable. Skylights could be put in, drastically changing the dim cabin into a cozy, well-lit place. And the bathroom—

His line of thinking startled him. He couldn't keep the cabin. It was entirely impractical. Why, it would take a good five, six hours just to fly there out of La Guardia. If he was going to have a vacation home, it should be in the Hamptons or in Martha's Vineyard or in Maine. Somewhere accessible.

He leaned his head against a peeled post. *Somewhere accessible.* The sheer inaccessibility of Montana had been surprisingly welcome. His phone had stopped ringing constantly. There was no television. He got his news from the *Daily Interlake*—though not quite the *New York Times,* a tolerable paper out of Kalispell—and what he could gather from Paul Harvey on the radio. There were stretches in every day when he didn't talk to anyone for an hour or more. There were other stretches when he paced the floor, actually bored and looking for something to do. And he liked it that way.

Jared hadn't missed his office or Manhattan or traffic or eighty-story buildings or Patricia. Not for a minute. And he was getting to something deeper within himself, something important there. The time away, the quiet, the river itself, seemed to speak to him, to call to him. He sat down heavily in an old leather chair, its seat split down the center. Shaking his head at the revelation that he was in no hurry to leave, he focused on the old paper on top of the stack. His hand began to tremble.

It was from his mother, written in the rounded loop of a young woman trying to please. He had very few written articles from her— a couple of letters to his uncle and aunt, who had become his guardians after the accident. Seeing her handwriting there, in that place, was like witnessing something holy. It was a breath of life from a long-dead past.

6/15/61

Dear Uncle Rudy,

I am sorry to ask this of you, but I have to. Rick and I aren't getting along very well, and I need some time away to think about the future. For me and for Jared. He's one now, and soon he'll be copying Rick, acting more like him. I don't want that to happen. Rick is back on drugs and can't hold a job. I'm working nights to make ends meet, but it's still not enough. I want

more for my boy. Can we come stay with you for a little
while? I think that some time on the river will help me
get my head on straight, give me some vision for the
future. If it wouldn't be too much of a burden, that is.
Let me know.

Love, Anna

The letter fluttered to the ground, and Jared scrambled back-ward a few paces, staring back at the note as if it would jump up and bite him.

It was a letter about bringing *him* here.

To the place she would die.

To the place where he would be saved.

Jared felt as if he were suffocating, smothering. He had to get out of the cabin. Right away. He had known she had died here, yet he hadn't anticipated encountering remnants of her. He had stared at the river, wondering about her death. The letter brought her alive again.

He walked quickly outside, taking a deep breath of the clean river air as if surfacing after being held under water. He was glad to be out of the musty, cramped living room, glad to have some distance from that letter. Coming across a deer path he had spotted beside the road, he walked, clambering over fallen trees, ducking under the occasional low branch, walking, walking as quickly as he could. It traced the river's edge, but the sound of the water faded into the background, his ears full of nothing but what he imagined was his mother's voice. She had come to this place seeking refuge, solace, direction.

Wasn't that exactly what he needed now? He and Patricia were through. His business was successful, so successful that he could apparently walk away for more than three weeks without even Don complaining too loudly. It startled him that he was so free, when his life had felt so constrained. Had he only imagined that he was so important at the office, that things would cease to work if he wasn't around? Was it all an illusion? He paused at a point in the path that jutted outward, across a gray-black granite cliff that stood strong against the July current. He looked down at the swirling, ice-cold waters as he did each morning on his run, wondering about his mother's last moments.

The river's water had the power to wash away the past—or bring it to the surface like a decomposing body released by a powerful spring surge. He shuddered, even though he knew his mother had not remained in the water for long. His aunt had told him the whole sad story. An old fisherman had seen them go in and rescued baby Jared, but apparently he could do nothing for Jared's mother.

What would Jared's life have been like had she lived? If the old man had rescued her, too? Would a younger man have been able to save them both?

The water bubbled and curled in small eddies, hitting boulders, winding around them. What had Anna's last moments been like? Had she been relieved, like a rushing river finding the freedom of plummeting over a towering waterfall? Glad for the end of a life that had turned into misery? Or had she been sad? Giving away her child to a stranger? So close to a safe haven, only to die at its door, like a stagnant pool, cut off from the fresh waters of its life source. There had been a hint of hope in her letter, a desire to see a life of happiness and security for her only child. She had cared enough to make her escape from Jared's father, a man who had long since disappeared, who might even be dead. She had cared enough to spirit her child away.

To the river. He closed his eyes, feeling a light spray of water against his windward cheek. "Mother," he whispered. Jared was surprised by the tears that sprang to his eyes and quickly brushed them away, looking left and right as if he expected as many people about him as at Times Square. He swallowed past the lump in his throat—it had been decades since he had cried for the mother he had barely known—and continued his walk, burying his hands in his pockets, his head tucked. His stomach rolled and bile rose, but the walk, the sounds and smells of the river, seemed to help, calming him.

And what of the old man? Who had he left behind when he gave his own life for Jared's? If Jared was half a man, he would seek the family out, confess who he was, tell them that he... What? Appreciated his life? Being here on the river, away from the chaos and stress of the city, had brought his life sharply into focus. He was estranged from a beautiful, wild wife. Again. His days in New York were immersed in mindless, easy work, in commodities—slippery, distant vehicles toward more money. His apartment was sparsely furnished, his refrigerator mostly empty. And his son, his wonderful son, lived miles away from him at school. Buckley was a fine establishment, but was that where he wanted Nicolaus to grow up? Without him?

On and on Jared walked—upriver, across the bridge, toward the lake, then finding another deer path, taking it. He walked through a grove of black cottonwoods towering one hundred and fifty feet above him, past their dark gray, deeply furrowed trunks that reminded him of curious old men, then through another grove of ten or twelve quaking aspens, a thousand shining, youthful leaves dancing in the wind. The sound was like that of crinoline and taffeta and silk brushing together sixty feet above, and he stared upward for a moment, lost in their movement. It was when he looked down that he discovered her.

She was sitting on the cliff above the river's beginnings, where the calm waters of the lake's end met the sucking demand of the narrowing waterway, near the bridge, amidst a small stand of birch saplings. She was barely visible, and he moved to one side in order to see her better, in order to offer a greeting, but he immediately fell silent. All he could do was stare, dumbstruck at the sight before him.

Eden Powell was not a beautiful woman. Shoulder-length, straight brown hair. Bushy eyebrows that arched over her closed eyes. She had a pleasant-enough olive complexion, but her nose was a little large, her chin a little too strong.

Yet her face was lifted to the sun, as if absorbing it, and she had the most exquisite expression. Utter peace and yet utter yearning at the same time. She moved a hand slightly upward, as if receiving something. Her lips spread in a tiny smile, which then faded. She was earnest, so earnest.

Fascinated, all Jared could think of was Renoir's painting, *Unrequited Love.* Her hands, with nails cut to the quick, remained open and slightly cupped, slowly dropping to her lap. Then one hand slowly went to her throat, as if she were hearing something. He found himself holding his breath, searching the immediate surroundings, listening to see if he could hear what she heard.

His eyes went back to her face. She was completely open, adoring, reverent.

It came to him then. She was praying. *Communing.*

And he was intruding.

He backed up, wanting to leave her special place, to leave her in peace. What would she think of him, staring at her when she was so vulnerable? He winced as he stepped on a brittle stick, breaking it in two with a loud crack.

Her eyes flew open, a bit dazed, then quickly narrowing in focus. "Jared!" She rose in one fluid motion, clearly startled, clearly displeased.

"Eden, I'm—"

"What are you doing here?"

"I was out for a walk. I didn't mean to intrude…"

"But you…" Her words faded as she looked at him accusingly. She had seen enough. Seen enough to know he hadn't come upon her and politely turned away. She knew the truth. That he had been staring at her.

He was the intruder, the interloper.

She looked upriver, then back at him. A red tide climbed each side of her face, from the neck upward. "I need to get going anyway." He winced at the disappointment, the hurt, in her voice. Eden turned, walking along the path back toward her home without a further word.

Jared started to call out to her, then shook his head. Anything he could say would sound ridiculous. The best thing to do was let her go. To try again later.

Anna carefully reviewed the things in her cart one more time; she wanted to make sure she had enough cash to cover the essentials, since she wouldn't be paid for another five days. Milk, rice cereal for the baby, eggs, bread, a five-pound bag of apples that were on super sale. It was enough. If she could get a couple of meals from her friend at the diner, they would make it through until payday.

The baby cooed at her and shifted in her arms, straining to see the brightly colored cans they walked past, then up to the fluorescent lights above. The sights, sounds, and smells of the store fascinated him, and Anna smiled and kissed his soft skin. They waited patiently in line, then unloaded the meager goods from their cart onto the cashier's belt.

She was a friendly woman—thin, tall, big smile. She leaned over the counter to tickle the baby under the chin, then continued to punch in the prices of the items Anna had chosen. Carefully Anna set the child on a small desk meant for writing checks and fished out her wallet.

"That'll be twelve dollars and twenty-two cents, honey," the cashier said. She looked at the baby again. "Aren't you just the cutest thing? Aren't you?" she asked in a high-pitched voice.

Anna heard it as if she were a mile distant.

Her wallet was empty.

Rick had been on a binge since losing his last job, and now he had robbed Anna of her grocery money. Feeling the flush of embarrassment climb her face, Anna looked the cashier in the eye. "I...I'm so sorry. I thought I had cash with me, but I think...I'm sorry. I have no money." She swallowed hard against the burning lump in her throat. She felt as *if she was on the verge of panic. What would they eat for the next five days? What was she to do?*

The cashier looked upon her in a kindly fashion. "Let me talk to the manager, honey. I think we have some shelf stocking that needs to be done. You could work off the groceries and go home to a full cupboard. The baby could play in a basket beside you."

"Really?" Anna asked, wiping away the tears that ran down her cheeks. "You'd let me do that?"

"Today only, sweetheart. My boss has a kind heart, but he doesn't want nobody to take advantage of him."

CHAPTER FIVE

One early July morning, Eden walked to her favorite fishing spot five hundred feet downriver from the new bridge. There was a terrific logjam at the bend of the river there, and the biggest trout often sought the shadows of the old, grayed remnants of trees. It was early, and she had just set up and begun casting when voices from upriver made her frown. She considered moving but was reluctant. This was her fishing spot. Hers.

The whir of her line whizzed by her head, and Eden smiled in satisfaction as it dropped within inches of the old silvered log and floated slowly across the deep, green pool beneath, just in the ripple where the trout couldn't see her. It was a perfect day, full of promise, solitude, and leisure.

She scowled as they came into view across the river, father and son, overdressed in their perfect vacationers' fly-fisherman gear. She was still angry with Jared for spying on her and didn't feel like sharing her fishing spot today. She picked up her fly box and moved downriver, then decided to switch flies.

"Hi!" Nicolaus greeted her brightly, his voice carrying easily across the water.

She flipped her head back and let a small smile spread across her face for the boy. "Hey, Nick."

"Catch anything?" he yelled again.

Eden cringed. She wouldn't catch anything with the kid carrying on like that. "You gotta be quiet or none of us will catch a thing," she told him kindly, gesturing to keep it down.

He looked appropriately chastised and nodded, and Eden smiled again. She never looked at his father.

She finished tying a brown Nymph to her line and then rubbed oil into the fly to keep it afloat. Pulling out a length of leader line, she eased the rod over her shoulder, cast forward, pulled it back again—not allowing the fly to drop—then forward and back, forward and back, feeling the rhythm of the line, listening to the pleasant *whir* past her ear. Gently she dropped the fly just where she wanted it, between two points of a boulder midstream.

Eden waded in up to her knees, pulling the line toward her, making the fly look alive to the fish below, concentrating on drawing them in. *Come on, baby. Come to Mama.*

"Now cast!" Jared encouraged Nick. "A little harder next time, buddy."

Eden winced. Fly-fishing was not about strength or throwing line out. It was all about placement. But she ignored the twosome, lifting out her fly as it drifted past any point of hope, letting it cross behind her, then gently setting it in the exact same spot again.

"No, Nick. Not like that. Put your shoulder into it."

That's it. "Excuse me," she called across the river. Both of them looked up. "I'm sorry...I couldn't help overhearing. It's not about your shoulder action. It should be easy, fly-fishing. Not such an effort."

"I...I think I've got it handled," Jared bristled.

Eden nodded and turned back to her rod. Once more she placed the Nymph between the two points of the rock, where both sides met in a waterfall, leaving the tiniest of fleeting pools between them.

Immediately a fish struck. With actions born of years of experience, Eden pulled the line taut and began to bring it in. She pulled a net from behind her back, landing the fourteen-inch trout in seconds.

Hooking her index finger under the gills, she took a look at her catch as she released the fly from the fish's jaw. After admiring the iridescent flesh, she gently let him go. He eagerly wriggled away. Eden stood, sighing with pleasure, then moved upstream. She sneaked a look across the river and knew that the Conways had watched the whole thing.

"A little harder this time," Jared encouraged Nick. Eden shook her head. Where *had* the man learned how to fish?

Reaching the point where the lake opened and the current sped up past the new bridge, she cast, watching as her fly moved downstream. It began to sink, so she lifted the line, easily letting it cross her shoulder, back and forth, the line arcing in a graceful dance, drying the fly, then she placed it again, right where she wanted it. A fish struck.

This time it was an eighteen-incher.

"Maybe Miss Powell can help us," she heard Nicolaus say to his dad. She hid a small smile.

"I'm sure she can. But we've got it handled. We'll be just fine. Just keep at it. Right there. Right where you put it before, Nick."

When Eden turned to go, offering them a small wave, they still hadn't caught a thing.

Nick showed up alone three days later, finding her fishing just around the bend from her cottage, right by the new bridge.

"Where's your dad?" Eden asked quietly, not wanting to scare the fish.

"Working on the cabin. I told him I was going to practice casting."

"Why practice? Why not fish?"

"Haven't been catching much. Might as well practice."

Eden laughed softly. "Want some pointers?"

"Sure."

"Come on over," she invited, tucking her head to her right as she pulled in line. The boy ran across the bridge and joined her.

"Fly-fishing is pretty basic. It comes naturally, if you just know a few things. Show me a cast." She watched the boy cast as if he were throwing a baseball. The line ended in a heap in front of him. "Okay. Let's start from the beginning." She ran him through a bunch of pointers, remembering the summer she'd been eight and her dad had taught her. "Keep your wrist rigid, straight, as if there were a bandage on it. Here," she said, bending over him. She tucked the butt of the rod into his sleeve. "That oughtta do it. Now, let your forearm do the work."

Nicolaus brought his arm back and set his fly perfectly, about fifteen feet out. "Wonderful!" she whispered, patting him on the shoulder. "Practice that for a bit."

They stood, side by side, casting for several minutes. Eden was wading outward, when Nick let out a *whoop*. "Pull her in!" Eden cried. "That's right! A little tighter!" She reached backward, bringing her net forward and scooping up the small trout. "Good work!"

Nick's grin spread from ear to ear. "Wait 'til I tell Dad!"

"No need," came his low voice from the bridge. "I saw the whole thing. Good work, Nick."

"It's all thanks to Miss Powell. She told me to keep my wrist straight. That's why I couldn't get any line out the other day."

"I see," he said.

"Trick I learned from my dad," she said. "He always used to tuck my rod into my sleeve."

"Good idea," he said, nodding. "Got any other advice for Nick?" he invited.

She glanced at him. "Sure."

"If you're willing, we'd appreciate it. I'll probably learn a few things myself." He climbed up onto the bridge railing, perching there like a crow on a telephone wire.

"All right," she said. What was it about him that made her so uneasy? She concentrated on the boy. "Put down your rod, Nick." Obediently, the child did as she asked. "Now, hold your hand up like you were holding a fork, with a chunk of potato on the end of the tines." Throwing her a *you're crazy* look, the child held up his fist. "Casting a line is a lot like throwing off a chunk of potato from your fork. Think of it like a food fight. Your target is about twenty feet out, right past that snag. See it? Now keep your aim, draw back your ammo a bit, good, *stop!* Yeah, like you're revving up. Now a short burst of speed and *stop!* There it goes! Sailing across the water. Get it? It's not about force. It's about a short burst of speed."

"I think I get it." Nick practiced a couple of times, then picked up his rod and did exactly what he had done with the imaginary fork. The line sailed out to about twenty feet.

Jared shouted his encouragement from the bridge, and Eden smiled. "There you go!"

"Thanks, Miss Powell!"

"No problem. I'll leave you to practice. I have to get to work."

"Oh, okay."

"You'll be fine, Nick. Just practice keeping your wrist straight and the whole potato thing. If you want to try something else helpful, come on over to my house someday. You can try a paintbrush exercise my mother taught me."

She nodded at Jared.

"Thanks for your time, Eden."

"My pleasure."

"May I walk you home?"

"No need," she said lightly. "I know the way."

She turned toward the road, feeling his eyes upon her back. Jared Conway was a dangerous man. Just as threatening to Eden as her would-be groom had been. Jared made her feel vulnerable, exposed. And she didn't like it one bit. Not one bit.

Jared hurried down the street in Bigfork, toward the small bookstore. He entered, inhaling the good smell of printer's ink. He'd seen the woman behind the desk before but was unable to place her. "Got anything on fly-fishing?" he asked.

"Right behind you, on the local interest table," she directed, letting her blue eyes fall to the paperwork before her.

He picked up a copy of *Essential Fly Fishing*. "This a good one?"

"It seems popular. You could ask down at Two River Gear what they would recommend."

"No, that's all right." A coffee-table book with beautiful photographs of Montana caught his eye, and he thumbed through it.

"Just visiting the Flathead?" the proprietor asked.

"For a while."

"How long are you staying?"

"Not sure yet. I inherited a cabin on the Swan River. I'm here to empty it out, as well as take a vacation."

"Ah, I see. Whose cabin?"

"Rudy Conway."

"Oh! You were related to Rudy?"

"He was my great-uncle."

"He was a good man."

"Yes, well, I didn't know him very well."

"That's too bad. My name's Sara Miller." She stuck out a hand and shook his firmly. "Your uncle was very kind."

"I'm beginning to see that," he said. "Rifling through a man's things gives you a sense of what he cared about. He cared about *a lot*," he said with a laugh. Sara laughed with him. "I'm Jared Conway."

"Nice to meet you, Jared." She pulled out a flyer from a Plexiglas holder on her crowded desk. "If you're looking for something to do, the Swan River Trio is playing here tomorrow night. Seems apropos, you being on the river and all."

Jared smiled. "Are they any good?"

"Pretty decent. The locals like them."

The locals. Suddenly he knew where he had seen Sara before. In a car with the gallery owner across the street, passing him on the bridge and turning into Eden's driveway. "Draw a lot of people?" he asked carefully.

"Quite a few," she said knowingly. "Come. Give 'em a listen. It's free."

"Thanks for the invitation. I'll see if my son wants to come. If so, I'll be here."

Anna crouched as the plate came flying over her head. Her grand-mother's china shattered into a hundred pieces. She knelt and then went to the floor as a cup and saucer followed. "Stop!" she screamed, weeping as the last tangible connection she had with her grandmother disap-peared forever. Jared was wailing just a few feet away in his bassinet. "Rick, stop!"

He threw another cherished piece in response, not himself, not any-one she knew anymore. "You prize your things more than me!" A drink-ing glass sailed over her head. The baby howled even louder. Anna reached out toward him but could not find the will to stand and shield him—she was too scared to move. She stifled a moan of fear as Rick walked toward her, his feet crunching through the remains of Limoges and Wedgwood. They were the only fine things that Anna had ever had, would ever have.

He leaned down, and Anna cowered, bracing for the blows that were sure to come, trying to stay still and hear him out to end this terrible moment but desperately wanting to break for help.

"Shut that kid up, or he's next," Rick said, his breath hot in her ear. He stood and kicked her in the side, stealing the wind from her. Then he left, off to find his next high somehow, even without any cash from her.

CHAPTER SIX

"Come tonight, Eden," Sara said across the phone lines.

"Who's playing?"

"Who else?"

"I love the Swan River Trio just as much as everyone else, but can't you get someone else for a change?" Composed of a guitar, drums, and vocal talent, the trio did a mixture of folk and pop music a couple of times a month at Sara's bookstore. Eden liked them very much, but she was in the mood for something…different.

"Sorry. We're not exactly the biggest gig in town. Most go to the Garden Bar. Come on. I need to count on a few regulars for these guys. There'll be coffee and cookies. And you can help me with Sheridan. I haven't been so busy with the summer crowds that I haven't missed you here in town. You're coming tomorrow, right? To Renee's for breakfast?"

Eden sighed. The idea of driving the fifteen minutes to Bigfork tonight *and* tomorrow seemed overwhelming. "I don't know."

"What?" Sara's voice was genuinely surprised. "Are you all right?"

"Fine, fine," Eden said hurriedly. "I'll be there. What time does it start?"

"Seven, as usual. Eden, you sound distracted. You sure you're all right?"

"I'm fine, Sara. I'll be there."

"Oh, good. 'Bye."

Eden said good-bye too and hung up the phone—a heavy, black, retro-dial model that she refused to dispose of. It had belonged to her grandfather. The weight of it in her hand felt good somehow, substantive. She stood there, staring at it for a moment, remembering her grandfather, who had died last year. She needed to get to the rest home in Kalispell and look in on Gram.

Her friends were right. She was turning into a hermit. It was time to get out of the cottage, away from the dead wildflowers wilting over the edge of a tarnished urn, away from the idea of Jared surprising her around every corner. Maybe an evening in town was just what she needed.

She was on the porch that evening, absorbed in her sculpture of the troubled woman, when she sat back on her haunches and really looked at her from top to bottom again. The vision she had seen in her dream was now nearly complete, from the tucked-under feet to the outstretched hand.

What was she afraid of? What made her so scared? Why had Eden been given such a vision?

She acknowledged for the first time that the woman might represent herself, perhaps God showing her that she'd been too afraid for too long, that she needed to reach out, even in the midst of her fear. Eden blew out a big breath and let her gaze leave the figure and go to the setting sun, casting out brilliant streams of gold and hot orange on the lake. She glanced at her watch. "Shoot!" She had intended to shower before going into town, and now there wasn't time. Quickly she washed her hands in the enamel bowl of water and hurried into the kitchen for a glass of juice.

Her eyes wandered to the brown, wilting flowers in the tarnished urn. She hadn't seen Jared running that morning and wondered if he might have packed up his son and headed back east. She pushed away the words in her head—*I hope not*—unwilling to admit they were true.

Eden hurriedly changed into a black, short-sleeved sweater and jeans, pulled on her black flats, then brought her hair back in a quick knot. After dabbing on a little makeup, she departed, sighing at the time, knowing her friends would say she subconsciously wanted to miss it. Leaving the cottage door and windows open to air out the hot rooms after a scorcher of a day, she went to her truck. When she turned the key, the engine rumbled but then stalled, as it was given to doing on occasion. Grimacing, she hopped out and raised the hood, fiddled with the starter, then tried again. It revved right up. After slamming the hood again, she was off to Sara's little concert, one of the few evening events in summertime Bigfork that did not revolve around booze or the playhouse.

Jared saw her arrive and moved behind the biography shelves in order to observe her for a moment and think of something to say. He watched as she greeted the bookstore owner, Sara, then the owner of the gallery across the street. In such a small town, it hadn't taken much detective work to discern that the three were close friends.

Eden walked with confidence and poise, and he noticed how her smile lit up her eyes when she reached for Sara's baby. She had a friendly face and an easy, inviting way about her. Dressed in slim jeans and a shirt that hugged her torso, she drew Jared's admiration. Chastising himself for setting himself up for another fall if she should discover him again spying on her, he decided to approach her.

When she handed off the baby and went to the punch bowl, he went too. She reached for a lemon cookie just as he did. She looked up then, surprised. He tried to lighten the moment. "We should stop meeting like this."

"Yes," she said, taking a bite of cookie and shooting him an unwavering gaze. "We should." He stared at her hand that held the cookie. Two of her nails were black, while the others were dyed a brownish cream. She followed his gaze. "My pickup wouldn't start."

"You started it yourself?" As the words left his lips, he knew he sounded condescending.

"Yep," she said wryly, adopting a hick accent and sliding her thumbs beneath imaginary overall straps. "We country women do a heap o' work out here in these parts. Even start our own engines, rather than wait upon some man to do it."

"Look, Eden, I'm sorry." He sighed, wanting to set things straight with her. "For that day on the river with Nick. For that day when I stumbled upon you. I'm not usually a bumbling idiot."

She raised her eyebrows and nodded slightly in agreement, her wry smile growing. "You're not?"

"No. Some women actually find me charming."

"Mmm hmm." She took a sip of punch.

"No, really." Why was he so drawn to her? Why make such an effort? The woman was clearly uninterested. Still, he pressed on, driven for some unknown reason. "Can we start over?"

"Start over?"

"Yes." He held out his hand. "Jared Conway. I'm a commodities broker from New York and am staying on the river with my son, Nick. You are?"

She considered him, and for a moment Jared wondered if she would turn and walk away. Her eyes told him that that was what she wanted to do. But after hesitating, she took his hand, her grip strong and warm, nothing like the limp society handshakes he was used to. "Eden Powell. Local artist. I live on the Swan."

Jared smiled, feeling a spark of hope inside. He knew why he was drawn to her. The woman before him was wholly, completely unique. *And ducking again behind some inner wall*—he could see her withdraw. She was actually turning away from him when the gallery owner walked up to them, wrapping a slim arm around Eden's shoulders.

"Are you ready for another exciting Bigfork evening?"

"Oh yes," Eden said. "Renee, this is Jared Conway, whom I've just met. Jared, this is Renee Scott, owner of the Electric Avenue Gallery."

Renee's big blue eyes turned toward Jared. "I'm pleased to meet you, Jared. Have you seen this woman's artwork?" She tilted her head at Eden.

"No, I—"

Renee laughed, cutting him off. "Sorry, Eden said you just met. You really should see what this girl does. She's incredibly talented." She took a cookie and then smiled. "I'd better get back to Sara and see if she needs any more help." She scooted away, leaving them.

"What kind of artwork do you do?" Jared asked.

"I'm a ceramist."

They nodded in tandem, an uncomfortable moment of silence passing between them.

"We should go find a seat," Eden quietly offered. She turned, and Jared took it as a half-invitation to sit with her. Not seeing Nick in the nearby aisles, he followed her to the back of the bookstore, which opened up into a large "living room" space, complete with old velour chairs and sofas, a hutch, a rocker, and a piano. The Swan Lake Trio was tuning up in one corner, with Nick right beside them, intently watching the guitarist. The room rapidly filled.

The bookstore owner waved Eden and Jared over while bouncing her baby girl on her lap. "Come! Sit! I think there's room for two." Eden hesitantly moved forward and sat primly on the edge, right next to her friend. There was barely enough room for Jared to squeeze in. He leaned backward into the fluffy pillow, trying to give Eden as much space as possible, conscious of her unease. Sara leaned back too, behind Eden. "Hi, there, Jared. Glad you could make it."

"Thanks for the invitation."

"I assume you've met my friend Eden?"

Eden did not turn. Was that a red flush at her neckline again?

"We've met."

"Good, good." Sara glanced at Eden, a touch of concern in her eyes, then turned to her baby as the musicians began playing, bouncing her in rhythm with the music.

Eden did not move the whole time the musicians did their first set. As soon as they finished, she applauded lightly, then rose, scurrying out of the room without explanation. Jared followed her with his eyes until Nick bounded over, a book in his hand. "Dad, can I get this? Michael said it was really good."

Jared took it from him and examined the cover, then the price. "I suppose so. If it'll actually keep you still long enough to read it."

"I will. I'm going to go see what else they have."

"Okay, but don't leave the store, Nick."

"I won't," the child promised.

"He seems like a nice kid," Sara said, slipping a bottle between her fussing baby's lips. "And that book he picked up is a good one."

"Glad to hear it. And yes, he is a good kid."

Sara nodded and looked up to watch Eden's approach back into the room.

Jared watched too, missing Sara's next question. He turned to see her expectant face. "I'm sorry. I'm a little distracted these days. What did you say?"

"Never mind," she said with a shake of her head and a small smile. "There seems to be a lot of that going around."

"What's going around?" Eden asked, gingerly sitting again.

"Distraction."

Eden looked at her friend, and Jared wished he could see her expression. She sat up a little more straight and then, for the first time, turned toward Jared. Her eyes searched his. "What's distracting you?"

He looked back at her, considering his answer, wondering at her feisty, direct question. "Memories, mostly. Digging through Uncle Rudy's stuff is bringing up some family history I didn't really stop to consider before coming here."

"What did you consider before coming here?"

Jared paused. "Not enough, apparently."

"Hmm," she said, letting her look linger. She was a bit intrigued; he was sure of it. But wary, it seemed to Jared, for reasons beyond his rude interruption at her prayer place or Nick's dunk into the river. There was something in her eyes that spoke of hurt and betrayal, however distant. He knew that look. He saw it in his own eyes every morning when he looked at himself in the mirror.

"Good morning," Eden greeted her parents from the porch. It was a sunny morning, mid-July, and they were up from Havre for a short visit, on their way to British Columbia.

"Hello, sweetheart," her dad boomed. After years of smoking, John Powell's voice was low and gravelly, the stuff that radio personalities were made of. It had taken his wife twenty years to get him to quit.

"Dad," she said, entering his arms for a hug and kiss.

"You look wonderful," her mother enthused from the other side of the car. Eden moved to her and embraced the diminutive woman. Mary backed away a bit, as if to get a better look at her. "Happy. It's been a good summer for you?"

"Yes, yes," Eden said, looking away. "Come inside. I have some coffee on and muffins in the oven that I had better keep an eye on."

"Still using that old oven, are you?" her mother asked.

"Yes. I love it."

They followed her inside, John carrying two small overnight cases. Eden supposed that they had become adept at packing for short trips. Ever since her father had retired from his job with John Deere last year, they had traveled nonstop.

"It's so good to see you two," she said. "I've missed you."

"Oh, we've missed you too," her mother said. "Do we have stories to tell!"

John sat down by the counter on a stool beside Mary, watching Eden pour coffee and pull the orange-cranberry muffins out of the oven. "We're going to get a few more trips in before our third grand-baby is born. Then we're going to move in with them for a while."

"Lucky them," Eden teased, sliding a mug of sweetened hot coffee over to him.

"You think they don't want us?" her mother asked, worried. Eden gave her her coffee, black.

"No, no. I was joking. I'm sure they'd love to have you. For a visit," she said, narrowing her eyes at her father. "Knowing how Dad is with kids, I'm pretty sure he's serious when he says he wants to *move in* with Paul and Susan."

"Oh, we'd never do that."

"I know, Mom. So, you're off to Alberta next?"

"Yes. Lake Louise, Banff, all that."

"Sounds wonderful."

"Yes, I'm looking forward to it."

"Come on," Eden invited. "It's perfect outside. Let's eat on the back porch." Her parents followed her through the door, and they all settled into Eden's comfortable padded furniture under the eaves. The lake was choppy and still dropping heavy waves on the beach. It promised to be a perfect day.

"Oh, I've missed this place," her father said, staring at the water over his coffee mug.

"I've missed having you guys around."

"We'll settle down after a while," her mother promised. "Have to get some of this wanderlust out of my veins. Then we'll be back around. It would be good to start looking for a little land, John."

"Land?" Eden asked.

"Yes. We'd love to build a little cottage like you have here on the lake. Just two and a half hours from Paul and right near you. We'd have a couple of extra bedrooms so Paul and his family could come and visit." She paused for a moment. "Would that be all right? Or is that a little too close?"

"Are you kidding? I'd love having you closer!" She paused and gave them a mischievous grin. "But maybe you had better make it on the other side of the lake."

"It would just be a summer home. Your father and I are still pretty attached to the people in Havre. But we could come up here for a couple of months every year."

"It might be the only time I get to see you two, what with your traveling and all."

Eden offered her mother another muffin, but she declined and said, "They're wonderful, Eden. You always have been such a fine cook."

"Sometimes. It's tough to get excited about cooking for one."

"But you make that wonderful bread, and these muffins are fabulous."

"Maybe I'm a good baker. Haven't experimented much with cooking."

"I think you sell yourself short. You're good with the barbecue, too. I've never gotten the hang of it, and your father refuses even to try."

"She'd rope me in," he said. "I'd never get away from the thing."

They smiled together and then stared at the water for a moment in silence.

"So, you haven't had a chance to dine with any eligible bachelors lately?" her mother inquired.

"No," Eden said, lowering her head to look at her with a silent warning.

"All right, all right," she said, raising her hands. "I was only curious."

"You have to get yourself out more," her father said, joining in on the old refrain.

"That's what everyone keeps telling me," Eden said.

"It's the only way to meet people," her mother said.

"More coffee?" Eden asked, rising. "I'll go and get the pot." She left them then, knowing they were likely sharing a worried glance. The old-maid daughter, squirreled away in a cottage on the lake. *Let them worry,* she thought. She had enough to carry without taking on the weight of their concerns, too.

It was an old Buick, ten years or more, but Anna didn't care. The sign said it ran, and the price was right. With the extra work she was now getting at the grocery store, she hoped she could manage the payments. If she could just keep Rick away from her cash.

It helped that he was sober again. She would have been happier about it if he wasn't so mean in his sobriety. She had packed her bags the night she discovered he had taken her grocery money. He had begged and pleaded with her to give him another chance, swore he wouldn't touch the bottle or use drugs again. So far it seemed he was keeping that promise—and making her pay for his misery in different ways.

She ran through the figures in her head again. If Rick could help a little with the payments—assuming he would keep his new job—they would make it. Anna smiled at her baby boy, who grinned back at her adoringly. "Jared, my sweet, I think we're about to be car owners!"

The thought of never taking a bus again certainly appealed to her. But better yet was the sense of freedom a car would give her. If Rick ever got too mean or dared to lay a hand on their child, she would have a means of escape. Lately escaping had become a regular fantasy—going somewhere peaceful and quiet where she could get her head on straight and have time to figure out where she wanted her life to go.

Anna thought again of the river she had often visited in her youth. It had been just such a place for her, the water glistening in the sun as it swished past. She thought of her Uncle Rudy, a kind, generous man. She would write him. As soon as she got home, she would write.

CHAPTER SEVEN

"But we're going back in a few days?" Nicolaus asked him for the thousandth time.

"Yes, Nick. I just have to take care of some things at work, and then we'll be back."

"I don't know why I couldn't just stay with the Sundquists."

Jared sighed. They'd been through this before too. "I just didn't feel comfortable with it, Nick. You're over there a lot as it is, and besides, your mom wants to see you."

The boy seemed to brighten a bit at the mention of his mother. He apparently didn't see all the unattractive things that Jared saw in Patricia, only the good things. Jared was glad for it. It would be good for them to spend time together. And it would give him a chance to put out the fire that seemed to be raging at Conway and Associates. Don had called him in a panic two days earlier, telling him he had to come home. Don had mishandled a premier client's account, losing over one hundred thousand dollars in three days. He knew the client would have a huge influence over others on their roster, and Don needed help to buy the firm some time to make a recovery.

The airline tickets had been outrageous, over fifteen hundred dollars each, but Jared saw no way around it. Truth be told, it had come at a good time for him. He needed a break from Rudy's cabin, the connection to his mother, and the disturbing feelings he felt awakening his heart when it came to Eden Powell. He needed some distance. And being called to the office to resolve such a critical matter reminded him of why he loved his work: He felt important, integral, vital to the team. He admitted to himself that it fed his ego. He had been a little hurt that they had lasted as long as they had without him.

When they landed and came off the plane, Patricia was there, bending to embrace Nick with all the apparent heartfelt love a mother could have for her son. She rose, still keeping Nicolaus close to her side. "You'll be here for three days?"

"Three, maybe four. You'll be all right with him?"

"All right? It'll be wonderful!" She turned to Nick. "I thought we'd go to the zoo and take a ferry ride. And I got tickets to *Lion King*. The critics have all raved about the stage show." She was at her best during short, activity-drenched visits. Even she knew that long-term parenting wasn't her bag. Jared supposed she truly missed their son, was honest in her love for him. She just wasn't cut out to be a mother in the traditional sense. Still, he hoped the two could connect on this trip; it would be good for Nicolaus.

"Cool," Nick said, clearly excited. But he glanced at his father. "You'll come get me?"

"Of course, Nick. You'll have a great time with your mother, then we'll hop a plane back to Montana for a couple more weeks." He bent and gave his son a big hug. "Be a good boy for your mom."

"Okay, Dad."

"I can't imagine what might be such a draw in Montana," Patricia said, shaking her head in mild disgust. "What do you find to *do?*" She turned Nick toward the exit, heading out to the parking garage, nodding once at her ex-husband over her shoulder as

Nicolaus began chattering about all he and Michael did to keep busy on the river.

Jared motioned toward his cell phone in case she or Nick needed him, then turned in the opposite direction to hail a cab to the office. It took him two hours to assess the history of the client's portfolio, four hours to help Don talk the client down from the ceiling, forty-eight hours to gain enough money back to convince the client to give them a few more weeks, and another day to dig through the piles on his desk.

He considered not going back. It felt good to be in the swing of things, to be the hero that saved the day at the office. But there was a pull inside him that could not be ignored. He needed to go back to the river. To finish cleaning out Rudy's cabin. And for something more.

"Another ugly morning on the Swan, eh?" Jared asked, startling Eden at her potter's wheel as she spun out a plate. It had been a week since the concert, and Eden hadn't seen him out running—hadn't seen him at all. It had felt like a reprieve to her, and she had almost hoped he was gone, any danger to her heart avoided. But now, see-ing him there before her, his sweaty black hair sticking to his fore-head in endearing curls, she was glad for his presence.

She smiled down at him from the porch and then looked up the lake, glass-smooth now at eleven in the morning, mirroring the green wooded banks on the far side, not a boat on the water. The sun was climbing high in the sky, and her porch was heating up. She wiped her brow. "Yep. It doesn't get any uglier than this." Eden glanced back at him, his T-shirt sticking to his chest and back. He rubbed the back of his hand across his forehead and leaned on one knee, his foot firmly planted on her front stoop.

"Haven't seen you for a while," he said.

Eden fiddled with the plate, smoothing an edge here, pulling another there. "No. I've been busy. I have an art show here at the end of the month."

"Oh? Just yours?"

"No. I'm an exhibitor. One of about thirty that set up on Electric Avenue to sell their wares." She glanced up at him again. "Where've you been?"

"We went to Glacier for a few days and fished the North Fork. I hired a guide, to make sure there were no more mishaps. Then I had to run home to New York to take care of a problem at the office."

Eden nodded. "Sounds exhausting. And fun."

"It was fun—the time with my son anyway. This place has been good for us. He goes to boarding school in New York, so I don't get to see him much."

"I'm sorry."

"For what?"

"That he has to go to boarding school."

"You shouldn't be. It's a good place. I went there myself."

Eden kept her eyes on the plate as she worked. "But you miss him. He must miss you too."

He didn't answer for a moment. "That's true. But you should see this school. It has the best of everything. Nick's doing great with his studies, and he plays field hockey like he was born to it..."

She looked up at him then, took in his expression as his words trailed off.

"You're right. I miss him. It's one of the things I'm thinking over while I'm here. Although his mother and I are divorced, I'm wondering if there's some way I could keep him home. Maybe work from the apartment some of the time…" He looked out to the lake, as if visualizing a home two thousand miles away, and Eden suddenly felt the chasm between them. What was she doing? She was right to avoid him. He was a transient. A divorced, searching man who could suck the life from her heart and then fly away again.

"Do you want a cup of coffee?" she found herself asking.

"Got any water?" he asked wryly.

"A little," she answered in kind. "Come in." She rose and met him at the screen door, wiping her hands on her apron. "Where is Nick now?"

"Hanging out with his friend, our neighbor Michael Sundquist. They've become inseparable. It nearly killed him to be away for a week."

"Mike's a good kid."

"He is." Jared looked around. "So, you make a living as an artist?"

"I get by."

"Where do you sell your pottery?" He neared her at the sink, looking around at the cottage as he did so, almost running into her. She tried to hide a sudden shiver that went up her arm and glued a smile on her face as she handed him the cool well water in a tall glass.

"Galleries, mostly. Renee has a table full of my stuff. There are others across Montana and into Wyoming and Idaho. My rep covers those."

"Good for you," he said, nodding. Then he turned away, looking around. "This is a nice house, Eden."

"Thanks."

Without an invitation, he wandered about, leaning over the couch to look more closely at a painting, then across an end table to look at her sculpture, one of only two pieces she had ever put out on display. It was of a woman looking upward, one hand on her cheek as if covering a lover's touch. Her other hand was cupped and open to one side as if ready to receive. Eden called it her Praying Woman. Jared glanced from it, to her, then back again. Eden hated the burn of the blush on her neck. She could feel it climbing upward. Jared would know that the Praying Woman was her. It was as though he were seeing her in the woods again, when she hadn't known he was there.

"So, what are you up to today?" she asked a bit too brightly, trying to distract him, desperate to pull his attention away from the sculpture.

"This is beautiful, Eden," he said softly, picking it up.

"It's just something I did in my spare time."

"No. Don't discount it. It's...soulful. Full of energy and life. Full of...you." The admiration in his voice was unmistakable. Eden dared to look him in the eye. There was a spark of interest there, the hint of intrigue, and a flash of surprise and wonder.

She took the sculpture by the neck and pulled it away from his warm hands, glad that the "troubled woman" she had done was stowed away in the storage shed. She set the small sculpture on the end table again. "Want to see the rest of the house?"

"Sure." He followed her through her office to her bedroom and upstairs to the studio. She could feel his eyes on her back more than on her walls now, however. Eden immediately regretted bringing him upstairs. He went directly to the far corner, evidently spotting all of the sculpted figures she had placed behind a heavy screen.

He picked up the figure of a boy lying backward on a bank with a long reed in his mouth, then a woman holding a child high in the air as if in offering. For a long moment he was silent. "Eden, do you sell these?"

She laughed hollowly. "No. Nobody's interested in those. They want usable stuff. Those're more for me."

"Why? I mean, why do you assume no one else would be interested in them? Why not assume that something that has so much of you in it would be intriguing?"

"I don't know," she said, a little exasperated. "I just do."

"I disagree."

"Excuse me?"

"You know, Eden. You know why you hide your sculptures back here."

"They're not hidden—"

"Sure they are."

"They're...*stored.*"

"Oh. Okay."

She stared at him for a long moment. Just what did Jared Conway want from her? What right did he have to barge in on her life and make her feel so...invaded? He returned her look for a moment, then gave her a small smile and said, "I'm going to go get my glass of water. I'll be right back."

"No, that's okay. I'll come with you. I ought to get back to work." She followed him down the narrow stairs.

"I was hoping you'd take a break. Give me a tour of the lake. I saw your Morley down there." He referred to her handmade cedar canoe. Greg Morley had become famous for the canoes he turned out every year from his small shop in the village of Swan Lake. "I saw one at the resort down the way. Caretaker told me they cost a pretty penny."

"I traded him some place settings for it."

"Must have taken a bunch of pottery."

"A lot. I think it was worth it though." She loved her canoe and was glad that Jared showed an appreciation for it. The urge to show her off in the water helped soothe some of Eden's unease with him. "I guess…I guess I could get away for a short trip," she allowed.

"Great!"

Eden smiled a little and led the way to the beach. He helped her right the canoe, then watched in silence as she scooped a spider out and dumped him on the rocky shore. "Grab a couple of life vests and the paddles from the boathouse, will you?" she asked.

Glad to have him gone for a moment, Eden slid the canoe into the water and ran her hands over her hair.

Jared returned, and Eden nodded forward. "She's all ready. Hop on in."

"Go ahead. I'll push us off and man the stern."

She glanced at him in surprise. "You canoe?"

"New York is not all city streets. Upstate has some beautiful lakes for canoeing."

She nodded, still reluctant to give up her customary seat in back. She often went out on her own, using a J stroke to paddle by herself.

"You know, Eden Powell, at some point you're going to have to give me a chance to be your friend. To trust me."

She looked at him quickly, paused for a long moment, then

passed him a paddle. "I've already been swimming in my clothes once, thanks to you."

"You won't go under again. Not if I can help it," he promised, holding the canoe steady behind her as she walked to the far end, hovering over three feet of water.

And Eden got the distinct feeling he was not speaking about an unplanned dunking at all.

Jared chastised himself for the way he'd said it. The last thing he needed was to make promises to some woman who was at once completely exasperating and utterly mesmerizing. As he dug into the water with his paddle, matching Eden's strong strokes from the bow, he felt the pull across his back muscles, down into his biceps and triceps. They paddled hard toward the center of the lake, and then Eden paused. Jared did too.

"I love this view. If I could put my cottage here, I would."

Jared smiled. He could see why. Nothing obstructed the view of the Swan Range from here, and the lake moved away from them in an optical illusion of a large *V*. In the distance a motorboat pulled a water-skier, and two jet skiers frolicked in its wake. The water carried to them sounds from all around—a logging truck on the highway, an intermittent chain saw, the *rap* of a hammer on wood, the gurgle of a boat motor as it sank and surfaced on the waves. There was the report of gunfire from the old gravel pit and then the echo of it across the lake as sound met mountain. And closer by, the hum of a strafing bee was usurped by tiny waves lapping against cedar planks. They sat there for five minutes, unmoving other than the occasional stroke from Jared to keep them centered on their view.

The depths drew him like a magnetic force, almost threatening to pull him overboard, and old silenced fears arose to the surface like air bubbles from the bottom. He stared at the green water, hypnotized by the streaks of sunlight severing the water like laser beams, disappearing far below. How deep was the water here? If they were to sink, drown right here, how long would it take for their bodies to reach the silty bottom? What else was down there? A shiver ran down his back, and Jared concentrated on the view down the lake again, focusing on the distant when the present overwhelmed him. It was a trick his uncle had taught him long ago. He cast about for something positive, to set his mind straight again.

"I like the smell of it," he said, inhaling the scent of moss and wet rocks in the sun, the hint of pine trees at the edge, the more earthy odor of immersed, rotting birch leaves.

"I know," she said, flashing him a smile over her shoulder. It lit up her eyes. "I would know this place blindfolded. Did you know that Alaskan salmon can travel for several years in the Pacific and then return home to the rivers where they were born to spawn?"

"I'd heard that."

"They usually get within a half-mile of their birthplace," she went on, "led entirely by smell. Each river is unique in scent because of different trees and plants and animals. Or rain levels. Something like that."

"That's amazing. Do you know a lot about everything, Eden, or did you watch the Discovery Channel last night?"

"Discovery Channel," she admitted sheepishly. "But it's interesting, no? Not only do they get so close to their birthplace, but they often arrive within days of the fish that were born with them."

"Incredible." The thought struck Jared that he, too, would be able to remember the smell of the Swan when they went back to New York. It made him suddenly lonesome—the thought of leaving, of being so far away.

"Come on," Eden said suddenly, digging into the smooth water and sending a small, bubbling eddy his way. He joined her, matching her stroke, his eyes taking in the sculpted muscles of her arms, the strength of her back. She was used to paddling on her own. The western bank of the lake crept past them as the Morley sliced through the water. As she dug deeper and faster, he could feel Eden's subtle challenge to see if he could keep up. The muscles in his upper arms and back burned, but he did not let up. He would meet her challenge.

"Here," she said, nodding to the right. A bay opened up, emerald in color and incredibly still. On the rocky point was a log gazebo, rustic and yet elegant. Beyond it, up the hillside, was a multimillion-dollar lodge made of huge logs.

"Wow."

Eden glanced back at him. "Not that. *That*," she said, nodding toward a partially submerged snag. Suddenly, the bumps on the end of the log were moving, diving off.

"Turtles!" he whispered back excitedly. His voice returned to normal. "I don't know why I'm whispering. I've already scared them all off."

She smiled, and they continued paddling around the tiny bay. She backstroked when they reached the outer edge. "Look," she said, motioning downward this time.

Beneath them swam a turtle, gliding on silken green water, eager to make his escape. But beyond him was a giant boiler and radiator. "What's that from?"

"I think there must have been a logging operation here once. See the old pilings for a dock?"

Jared could see them now, amidst the crowded underbrush of the bank.

"They abandoned it? Just shoved it all down the hill?"

"Or it collapsed. Maybe it was on the old dock, in a boathouse. Went in on its own. I don't know."

Jared squared his shoulders after another shiver ran down his back. He was overanalyzing everything, thinking about the water—and going under—too much. "I'll have to bring Nick back to this bay. He'd love the turtles, the radiator. Can we borrow the canoe sometime?"

"Anytime." She began paddling again. "Let's stop over there." She gestured toward the million-dollar abode with the gazebo and state-of-the-art dock. He followed her lead, and they pulled alongside the wooden structure. Eden rose and eased onto the dock.

"You know these people?" he asked.

"Yes. Come on. I need to do something." She pulled a key from her pocket as Jared tied up his end of the canoe and followed her up the grassy bank and to the deck of the house. Eden unlocked the sliding door and let them in. It was classy, as beautifully decorated as if Ralph Lauren had just departed. He let out a long, low whistle. "Where are the owners?"

"Connecticut. This is their vacation home. I look in on it every once in a while, make sure everything's in order. Pete Fisher, the sheriff, trades off with me."

"Guess when you have a place like this, the sheriff will make house calls for you, huh?"

"Every month Pete looks in on every uninhabited cabin on the lake." Her tone told him she did not care for his inference. "We try to help each other out here." She disappeared down a long hallway and a couple of minutes later reemerged. "No mice. Nothing out of order. We can go."

"I'd like to stay for a few months."

"It'd be nice, huh?" she said, raising an eyebrow. She waited at the door for him to exit, then firmly shut it behind him. What would Eden think if she knew he could buy the place? He didn't think such things would matter much at all to her. She seemed to be a person who could be content anywhere. Not like Patricia. He stopped himself, surprised that he would make such a comparison. Jared went to the railing of the deck and ran his hands across the log that formed the top rail, over the bumpy knots and curves that had been smoothed with sandpaper, staring down the lake at the sun-drenched velvety mountains of the Swan Range.

"Now for the boat," she said, interrupting his daydreaming.

"The boat?"

"Gotta get it running. The Bakers arrive next week with a bunch of kids. They have two of their own, and they're each bringing two friends. They'll all want to ski. When the boat sits for so long, it tends to not want to start. Brandon Baker asked me to make sure it was ready, and if something was wrong, to call a boat mechanic."

"It looks brand-new."

"Guess they don't make them like they used to."

He followed her down the grassy slope. "Who taught you about engines?"

"My dad. He worked for years as a mechanic for John Deere,

then worked his way up in sales. He just retired last year. He and my mom are traveling everywhere they've always wanted to go. They stopped by last week on the way to British Columbia."

"Must be nice to have them near."

"Yeah. Even though I don't see them much. They're talking about buying some land here and building their own little cabin." Eden unsnapped the cover and rolled it back, then hopped into the boat and pulled out a set of wrenches from beneath the driver's seat.

"That would be nice."

She opened up the boat engine cover. Jared sat down on the dock to observe. "It would be," she agreed. "They said they'd build a couple of extra rooms so my brother's family could come up and stay."

"That'd be great."

"Where is your family?" She kept her head down, tightening a bolt here and there, emptying the oil into a pan and then retrieving a fresh bottle from the front.

"My mom died when I was little. I never knew my dad."

She looked up at him quickly, her eyes filled with pain. "I'm sorry, Jared."

"Oh, that's all right. I was raised by my aunt and uncle in Connecticut."

"Do you see them very often?"

"Christmas, the occasional Easter. Life has gotten…busy."

"You had cousins you were raised with?"

"Two. They both ended up in California, so I usually only see them a couple of times a year too. But they're good people, more like siblings than cousins. We keep up via e-mail. You have brothers and sisters?"

"That brother in Missoula. That's it. Paul has two kids and one on the way. And I love his wife. She's like a sister to me." She rose and tried the engine. It started up with a gentle *purr,* and she grinned.

"They pay you to do this?"

Eden threw him a funny look. "No. They're my neighbors. Remember? We try to help each other out around here."

"Of course. Sorry."

"No problem," she said, hopping into the boat. "You can work off your penance by letting me tow you."

"Tow me? In the canoe?"

"No. On skis. Want to go for a run?"

"How do you know I ski?"

"Don't you?"

"Yes."

"Then let's go." She turned and flipped the blower and bilge pump switches on the control panel, then moved on to the front of the boat. She reached under a seat and pulled out a bright blue life vest, then tossed it to him.

"You're serious."

"Absolutely. Why would you say no?" She waved toward the lake. "Glass. It's perfection." She was daring him, testing him.

"Because I'm nearing forty and I remember the sore muscles after a ski. Maybe another time."

"Ah. You're saying you're old?"

He clenched his lips. Again the challenge. "I'll show you how it's done one of these days," he said with bravado. "Maybe I can bring Nick over and we can teach him, too. If he's ready." Jared looked down into the water. *If it's safe.*

"Suit yourself," she said, a little disappointed. She turned off the blower and bilge pump and pocketed the key, then covered the boat with taut canvas that snapped to the sides.

They climbed back into the canoe, and Jared thought back to the last time he had skied, probably fifteen years ago or more. His family had often vacationed on a lake in Vermont with his aunt and uncle. They had pushed him to pursue any sport he wanted but especially encouraged anything with water—polo, skiing, swimming, diving. It had never occurred to him why. His cousins hadn't been pushed the same way, one taking on cross-country running as his sport, the other golf. He had always chalked it up to his aunt and uncle being busier, older when they were born, not having as much time in the summers when his cousins arrived home from Buckley. But as he stared at the lake, Jared knew it had been something more. Suddenly it just clicked, being here, so near the river. They had wanted him in the water as if they feared he might grow up with a phobia about it. *Get thrown from a horse, get back in the saddle.*

But that was ridiculous! They hadn't even told him how his mother had died until he was seven or eight. There was no way he could've remembered that day. Could he? Jared supposed there was probably a chance, even as young as he was when the tragedy occurred. Had they really been afraid? Afraid that he would be limited in some way by the trauma from the bridge? He had become adept on the water but never truly comfortable. He looked good on water skis, but he never really enjoyed it. *Like my life in general,* he mused, clenching his lips. *Looking good but never able to jump right into the river of life with abandon.* He remembered Eden that day on the cliff among the trees, the look of enchantment and wonder and awe on her face. What would it be like to feel, really feel, such powerful emotions?

"Jared?"

His eyes raced back to Eden, who looked over her shoulder at him.

"What?"

"I asked if you wanted to stop at this little island."

"Oh, sure."

"You still here with me in Montana?"

"I am now," he admitted. "Thinking about several summers I spent in Vermont. And other things."

She didn't say another word, simply continued to paddle toward the tiny outcropping of land covered in trees. "What's it called?" he asked.

"Goose Island."

"Why?"

"I'll show you."

Jared paddled hard with Eden. This was Montana, not Vermont, he reminded himself. And whatever his aunt and uncle wanted to pass on to him, it was all right with him. Hadn't he turned out okay? They had done their best; the rest was up to him. The canoe crunched on the rocks of the island. Eden didn't let it scrape for long before she hopped out, sacrificing her dry shoes rather than the prized Morley.

She led him among the trees to a giant nest of twigs on the ground. She knelt and picked up a broken shell.

"Goose Island," he said with a smile.

"Yep. Every year we have a couple of Canadian geese raise a nest full of adorable little goslings. They come swimming past my dock every spring, and it reminds me that summer is really on its way."

He nodded, smiling at her obvious pleasure. "They must know the way here like those salmon know their way back to Alaska."

"From Mexico to Montana every year."

They smiled at each other for a second, until it became awkward. "I had better head back," Jared said. "Nick's probably wondering where I went." Truth be told, the boy probably had no idea he was gone, nor would he even care. He was playing with Michael, and Jared was definitely coming in a distant second these days to the almighty Michael. But there was something happening between him and Eden that made Jared at once want to spend hours with her and yet at the same time gain some distance, perspective. He had to be careful. For both their sakes, he felt.

They paddled home to Eden's and climbed out at the dock. She tied the canoe against the cleats there and followed him up the grassy bank to her cabin.

"Thanks, Eden. That was great. I'm going to take you up on that offer to bring Nick over for a ride one of these days. And maybe we could borrow the Bakers' boat for that ski?"

"Sure. They're always willing to give others a pull."

He turned to go, then stopped. On impulse he said, "Eden… would you care to have dinner with us tonight?"

"Oh…I don't think so. Not tonight."

"Oh, okay. What about tomorrow? We could bring dinner over here, early enough so we could teach Nick to ski beforehand."

"Well, maybe."

"Terrific," Jared grinned, ignoring her obvious trepidation. "We'll see you about four o'clock. Thanks again for today."

"You're welcome," she said, a bit of wonder in her eyes.

He smiled at her and left. It was a good plan. Nick would love it.

*When Anna pulled the mailbox open that day, she was careful to keep
her black eye turned away from old Mrs. Judson, her nosy, disapproving
neighbor who often whispered with old Mrs. Barfunkle about Anna
and Rick "living in sin" and made sure Anna could hear. She hadn't
expected more than the usual coupon books from the Piggly Wiggly or
other junk mail. Her letter to Uncle Rudy had been sent weeks ago, a cry
for help that went unanswered. But then there it was, an envelope
addressed in his distinct writing and bearing her name. It was lucky
that she had picked up the mail that day instead of Rick.*

    *Trembling with excitement, she pulled Jared into her arms—he had
been crawling around and around a sprinkler head as if it were a
Maypole—and hurried into the apartment building, up the stairs and
past the feuding O'Kellys and Mr. Maple's loud TV. Reaching their
third-floor flat, she fumbled with the key, her hands shaking, so eager
was she to get inside and read her uncle's response.*

    *Setting Jared down in front of the television, she tore open the enve-
lope like a marooned, starving woman tearing through the peel of a rare
tropical fruit. She read the words quickly, grinning from ear to ear and
letting out a tiny squeal. Then covering her mouth, she read them more
slowly. The words of love and honor and welcome seeped into her soul
like healing oil from an anointed priest's hand. She had never had much
time for God, but lately she was learning to listen for his voice. He com-
forted her in those lonely hours. And now he had clearly made a way for
her. For Jared. To leave this place and find themselves again.*

The noise of the television set, Jared's jabbering, and the O'Kellys' fighting faded away. It was as if Anna were on holy ground, so near was God. She lifted her chin, not seeing the dingy, water-stained ceiling. She was looking up, up into the light shining down into her soul as clearly as a streetlight illuminated a homeless woman on a dark, lonely night. And there was joy, pure joy on her face as she welcomed him in, into her home, into herself, into her future.

CHAPTER EIGHT

"Why?" Nicolaus railed. "Why do we have to go over there?"

"Come on, Nick," Jared said, trying to keep his voice down. "I know you want to go to town with Michael, but tonight I want you with me. We'll have fun."

"But, Dad, we were going to the movies—"

"Which you can go to anytime, anywhere. Eden promised to give you a chance to water ski, and maybe we could have a bonfire—"

"Can Michael come with us?'

Jared sighed. "No, Nick. Tonight it's just the three of us."

Nicolaus looked at him with the awakening of suspicion in his eyes. "Why?"

"So we can get to know one another."

"Why do you care about some lady on the lake?"

"I just do," Jared hedged, turning away from his son and running his hand through his hair.

"She's not even as pretty as Mom."

"No, she's not."

"And she dresses like a boy."

"Not all the time," he said, thinking of her that night in town.

"You're not getting all mushy over her, are you?"

"No, Nick, I'm not getting all mushy over her. She's just a new friend."

"Then why do I have to go? Why don't you just go?"

Jared stared hard at his child. "Because I want you to get to know her. She's just a new friend, like Michael's your friend. Because this will be *fun*," he said through gritted teeth, already laughing at the paradox of his word choice and tone. He reached out to tickle Nick, to tease him out of his foul mood. Maybe it would be better to let him go with Michael's family to town… He shook his head. It wouldn't do to show up alone tonight. It might seem like a date. And neither he nor Eden was ready for that.

Nick dodged him and ran partway to his room. "Can we go see the movie tomorrow night if I agree to go to Miss Powell's? I really wanna see it, Dad."

Jared placed his hands on his hips. "You need to go tonight because I've asked you to do so. To be a good kid. Got it?"

"Yeah," Nicolaus said, hanging his head.

"But, yes, we'll catch the movie tomorrow night."

Nick immediately perked up and smiled. *"Yes!"*

"Go tell the Sundquists thanks for the invitation, but you can't make it."

"Okay," Nick agreed, rushing out the door. It slammed behind him, making Jared wince. But at least he was going with him tonight. And without the foul mood.

Eden stared across the bonfire at Nicolaus Conway. He was poking the coals with a long stick he had denuded of branches, intent upon making it a "spear." The boy had arrived with some suspicion in his eyes, some new, unexplained distance in his manner, but through the late afternoon of skiing lessons, the exhilaration of finally making it up, the canoe ride, and dinner, he was loosening up again. He was a good kid—polite, kind, and all boy. She could see why Jared was crazy about him.

"Want a marshmallow, Nick?" she asked.

Nicolaus's green eyes, so like his father's, immediately stretched wider and focused on her. "Yeah!"

"Better yet, let's make s'mores."

"Okay!"

"Come up to the house with me," she invited, standing. "Your dad can mind the fire while you help me gather the supplies."

"Okay!" he repeated.

Jared looked up at her with a smile as she passed, and she felt warmed by it. There was a glint of gratitude in his eyes, the touch of appreciation in the lilt of his lips. She stumbled over a stone step in the dark.

"You all right, Miss Powell?" Nick asked.

"Fine, I'm fine," she said. "And, Nick, you can call me Eden."

"Need my flashlight?" Jared called up to them.

"No thanks," she said. She had only climbed the steps a thousand times in the dark! What was wrong with her? She opened the door and led the way into the kitchen. In short order, she had found chocolate bars, graham crackers, and marshmallows. Nick turned to go with his tray.

"Wait."

"For what? It's all here."

"Nope. You need peanut butter."

"Peanut butter? For the s'mores?"

"Yep. That's how we Powells make 'em."

"Sounds gross."

"Try it. If you hate it, you can go back to the traditional way."

"All right," the boy said, not sounding at all hopeful about the idea. He turned away, carefully balancing the tray full of goods.

"You okay with that?"

"Yeah."

"You go ahead. I'll bring down a couple of blankets and some hot tea."

"All right." His focus was on the tray, not her words, as he tried to turn the knob.

"Here, let me get that." She hurried over and slid open the door.

Nick looked up at her with earnest eyes. "Eden?"

"Yeah?"

"Are you in love with my dad?"

Eden laughed. "No. Why do you ask that?"

"Just wondering. He said he's not in love with you either. He said you were just a friend."

"I…see."

"Someday he and my mom are going to get back together."

"Oh," she said softly, nodding a little. "I bet you'd like that."

"Yeah. They got divorced three years ago, but they almost got back together right before we came here. I figure it's just a matter of time," he said, shrugging his narrow shoulders. "Coming back down?"

"Yes." She looked away, trying to focus. "I'll just grab a few things and be right there."

"See you at the beach."

She closed the door behind him, made it back to the kitchen, then leaned her head against a doorjamb. *What are you doing, Eden? What are you thinking?* The boy's comment shouldn't have dug in like it had, hurting her. Of course Jared Conway was only interested in her as a friend. What else did she expect? They were here for a season, then heading home. Home—two thousand miles away. And her home was here. What did she expect? That somehow love would blossom?

It was all Renee's fault. And Sara's. All their fault for planting fanciful hopes in her head. She set the pot of water on the stove with a *bang*. God had placed her here for a reason. This was her place. She just couldn't be anywhere else.

She rubbed her eyes until they hurt. What...*what* was moving within her? She felt ill-at-ease, confused. She laughed mirthlessly. Not that she could change anything. Jared Conway thought of her as a friend. And not anything more. Eden pulled out a few tea bags from her earthenware pot, her mind fast-forwarding sixty years. She had been born on Montana soil, and she would die here.

Most likely alone. *You better keep reminding yourself of that,* she told her heart firmly.

"So, he stayed for dinner and then for a fire on the beach?" Renee asked, her arms crossed. She sipped at her cup of coffee, all the while keeping her eyes trained on Eden, who was sitting at the kitchen table across from Sara. It was a cold, rainy morning. It had stormed all night—beginning the moment Jared went home, it seemed to Eden.

"He and his son," she corrected. "It was a friendly, neighborly kind of thing."

"Uh-huh," Sara said knowingly. "Why get all starry-eyed then?"

Eden stuck out her tongue at her friend. "Maybe because I'm thinking of the stars last night."

"Or the stars in your eyes every time Jared got near you," Renee interjected.

Eden abruptly pushed back her chair, the legs scraping against the pine planks. "Enough. We have a friendship going—he's not interested in more." She walked away from them to look out at the lake, moodily gray and still, pockmarked by raindrops. "Nicolaus told me."

"Told you what? That his dad was only interested in you as a friend?" Renee asked. "Do you really think a man would tell his eight-year-old that?"

"I do, if the eight-year-old was worried about me getting in the way of his mother."

Renee clamped her lips shut. Eden felt a small victory even as the melancholy covered her as completely as the low clouds that covered the valley. She shook her head. "They just divorced."

"I thought it was three years ago," Sara said.

"It was. But they were apparently trying to reconcile. Nick told me yesterday that they just called it quits again, right before he and Jared came to Montana."

"Maybe that's what Jared's thinking about every time we pass him on the bridge."

"Speak of the devil…" Renee whispered.

Jared, his dark hair wet and shiny with rain, gave them a little wave. He opened the door uninvited. "May I come in, or is this girls only?"

"We can make an exception," Eden said softly. "I'll get you a towel." She left to grab a soft terry-cloth towel from the bathroom, her ears pounding as she strained to hear what the three would talk about.

They made polite conversation for a while before Renee asked, "Jared, why do you always stand on that bridge, looking like you want to jump in?"

There was an awkward silence for a moment. Then he said, "It helps me, somehow. To stand there and think." He looked up at Eden as she reentered the kitchen, and his eyes never left her. "It's like I haven't had time or space to think in years, and I have all this catching up to do."

They were quiet. Eden handed him the towel, trying not to drop her eyes but continue to meet his intense gaze. There was a hint of sadness in them. Did he think about his ex-wife as he stood upon that bridge? "Don't you move off that rug until you stop dripping," she said, trying to lighten the moment. "You want some coffee?"

"Water, please." He glanced at her friends, a small smile on his face, while she poured a glass for him. "Eden, yesterday was great. Thanks for everything. Nick had a great time too. He went to sleep last night talking about water skiing and woke up this morning talking about the s'mores. With peanut butter. You won him over. As if the fishing lesson hadn't done it already."

Renee shot her a knowing glance, and Eden narrowed her eyes, responding with a warning look.

"He was wondering if he could come over today for another one. A lesson, I mean. He said you had mentioned a paintbrush…"

Eden turned away. "Actually, today's not good. I have to finish an order for one of Renee's customers—"

"That isn't…" Renee's words faded away as she caught Eden's expression.

"And there's some paperwork…I have some paperwork to do," Eden continued awkwardly, turning back to Jared. "Maybe another time?"

"Yeah, sure," he said, a look of confusion on his face. He took a deep drink of water. "Sure. Well, listen, I'll head out and quit dripping on your floor." He turned to go.

"Jared," she said, following him, feeling badly now about hurting his feelings. "I want to float the Middle Fork of the Flathead River next week. Tell Nick to come over in a couple of days, and I'll give him that lesson. If you want, you two could join me on the float."

"Yeah. Okay. Let's see how it goes." His eyes searched hers for a long moment. Then he looked up at her friends, his tension easing into a bright grin. "See y'all."

"'Bye, Jared," they said, unusually still as they stared in Eden's direction.

Rather than face them right away, she followed him out onto the porch and down to the front yard. Jared leaned down and picked a delicate bluebell, then rose, ran thick fingers past her temple, tucking her hair back and gently placing the flower behind her ear. As if he had done it a thousand times before.

"Good-bye, Eden," he said, his eyes searching hers.

"Good-bye, Jared," she said, catching her breath.

He turned and ran up her driveway, then down the road toward the bridge.

Mother would not approve, Eden thought, her mind racing back to her hot, ill-fated wedding day, the day her father had come into the bridal room and broke the news that the groom would not be attending. Her mother had cried as if it were she who had been stood up, she who wasn't love-worthy. She shook her head. Jared Conway was dangerous. How stupid could she be? Why was she letting even the tiniest part of her heart loose to wander? To explore? A man like Jared Conway could trample it, kill it.

She stepped back inside, holding the bluebell in her hand, and was greeted by her friends' insistent questions.

"Stop, stop!" Eden said. "I don't know why I put him off. I just had to."

"What are you scared about, Eden? He's wonderful! Get to it!"

"Renee, it's not that easy."

"Sure it is. The man's hanging out, stopping by with excuses to see you. He's primed!"

"I don't think he knows he's stopping by for any reason other than to secure another free fishing lesson for his son. He's not ready for a relationship."

"He's ready for something," Sara said softly.

"Maybe I'm not." Eden sank down into her leather chair by the fire. The logs periodically spit out pitch, which sizzled and then caught fire like sparklers. But she barely noticed it; all she could see was Jared's handsome face and the tiniest bit of hurt in his green eyes. "He's too handsome," she murmured.

"For what? For you?" Sara asked. She came over and sat down on the couch across from her. "I think he's searching. For some kind of answers."

"Maybe he's trying to figure out what went wrong with his marriage," Renee said, joining her on the couch.

"I get the feeling that it's something deeper," Sara said.

Eden sighed. "He's too handsome *and* too complicated."

"Eden Powell, there's not a person alive out there older than twenty who doesn't have something from the past to deal with," Renee said.

"No. Sara's right. There's something more. He's looking for something more."

"Yeah. You," Renee said.

"No."

"Is it that foreign a concept? That you might be attractive?"

"I hardly look like you," Eden said, rising to get more coffee.

"You don't need to look like me. You're different. Earthy. Fresh. Clean. The more people get to know you, Eden, the more people discover how beautiful you are. Jared's discovering it."

"He's not."

"He is. You can see it in the way he looks at you. Think of it! Mr. Big City comes to the valley and discovers a treasure right across the bridge. You're probably all new to someone like him."

"And all wrong."

"Or all *right*." Renee leaned forward. "Don't run away, Eden. Give it a chance. Sure, it's risky. But what you might discover could be well worth the risk."

"He only thinks of me as a new friend," Eden tried once more.

"If that's true," Sara said, "it won't be long before he thinks beyond it."

Jared ran home through the rain, thinking of Eden as he tucked the flower behind her ear—her eyes so frightened, so wary. Why had he done such a thing? He paused at the bridge and then turned onto the deer path that led to the place where he had discovered Eden praying. He reached it within minutes.

The river was dark and angry-looking as it reflected the clouds' gray depths. He walked through the grove of cottonwoods to the stand of birch beneath the quaking aspens. The rain ceased to pelt him, the broad aspen leaves above protecting him. He did not sit down, for the grasses were wet from the night's rain, but he gripped a slender trunk in each hand, staring, staring at the roiling waters below him. "What is happening here?" he whispered, his words nearly drowned out by the sounds of the river. He looked up at the yellow-green leaves of the birch, up past them to the towering cottonwoods, beyond them to the gray skies. "What is happening to me?" he asked.

Eden had clearly been praying here, here in this sacred circle. Why couldn't Jared feel what she had so clearly felt? How did she become so close to a distant God? Father Frank had always told the boys at Buckley that God was right beside them. "Knock and the door will open," he often would repeat. But whenever Jared knocked, there was never an open door. Not that he had ever really been ready for it, he admitted to himself. And maybe he hadn't knocked loudly enough...

Did Eden find answers here, direction?

Because suddenly he felt as if he were on a river skiff without a paddle.

He had come here for a new start on his relationship with Nick and a break from his life. For a quick real estate deal. But all he felt was more and more torn up inside, staring nose to nose at himself, a man he didn't really care for. Drawn more and more to the mother he had never known. Sorrow furrowed his brow. He looked upstream to the bridge, the "new" bridge, as old as he. Someone had told him the old one had been torn down soon after the accident.

What had it been like for her, for his mother? To know she would die, that she wouldn't see her son grow up? His thoughts flew to Nicolaus, and his eyes misted over. Distantly he could hear himself sobbing, but he didn't care. What would it be like to hand Nick over to some old stranger, knowing he could do nothing to protect his son? He was lost in the image, the agony of powerlessness.

"I've tried to live a good life," he said to the sky. To his mother, to Eden's distant God. All he got in response was the empty, familiar rippling of the river. He paused, considering the water again. His mother had loved it here, clearly thought of it with good memories. For as much as the river had taken her life, it had given Jared up, birthed him anew into a boy who would be shaped to be tough and strong and stalwart. Self-sufficient.

He looked around again. Just where would he find the things he was missing? The things that he wanted to give to his son? Jared turned and walked out of the grove, breaking into a run again as he headed home. He couldn't put his finger on it, but he wanted something more, something he had glimpsed in Eden. Not just peace but something else…

When he reached Rudy's cabin, he pulled open the door and greeted Mrs. Sundquist. "Thanks for staying with him," he said. "I really appreciate that you're willing to do it."

"I've told you a hundred times it's no problem," she said, laying a warm hand on his forearm. "Gives me some peace and quiet. Your boy sleeps like the dead, and I get some knitting done."

"Would you care for a cup of coffee? I think I have some, some-where."

"No, no. I'll just get on home and start some breakfast for Michael."

"I'm sure Nicolaus will be up shortly."

"No doubt. Send him over to play in an hour or so. I'll be glad to keep an eye on them."

"Thanks, Mrs. Sundquist." He closed the door behind her, resolving to buy his neighbors dinner at a nice restaurant in Bigfork as thanks for their help in watching Nick. They honestly seemed to enjoy it, which helped assuage his guilt, but he still didn't want them to think he was taking them for granted. Just as he turned and headed to the phone to pick up his messages, Nick opened his door, rubbing his eyes.

"Good morning, Son," he said, forcing brightness into his voice.

"Dad," the boy said sleepily. He trudged into the kitchen and automatically poured himself some cereal.

Smiling, Jared turned back to the answering machine, fast-forwarding past several unanswered messages from Patricia. He wished they were from Eden. The thought sent a twinge through his body, as if he were disloyal for thinking about another when just weeks ago he was hoping to get back together with his ex. Did he even have what it took to fund a real relationship? Maybe he was only cut out for the kind of thing that Patricia and he had going— that superficial, tiresome, chasing game.

He sat down heavily in an old leather chair. Dust *poofed* up around him, and he grimaced. It was time to finish cleaning this cabin and be done with it. To let go of Patricia once and for all, find out what he could about Rudy and his mother amongst the stacks, prepare the cabin to sell, and return home. Out with the old, in with the new. But this self-talk did little to lift his spirits. His thoughts went back to Eden's sacred grove, to the troublesome thought that he was missing something, something vital. It was the same feeling he got when he was about to move forward with a deal but didn't know all the relevant details. He had to find out more. About this place, the river, his mother, the old man, Eden. He had to know more about the past in order to move forward with the present.

"Interesting," he murmured.

"What?" Nick asked, shoveling a spoonful of Cheerios into his mouth.

"Oh, nothing," Jared said, surprised to be caught in his reverie. "Saw Eden this morning. She wondered if we wanted to float the Middle Fork of the Flathead with her next week."

"That'd be fun," the boy allowed.

"Yeah, it would," he nodded. Eden was curiously linked to this river, his past. He saw her again in his mind's eye—amid the birch, completely open, completely reverent, completely joyful. With a start he realized he had come to hope that she would be a part of his future too.

Anna rolled over and looked at the clock again. Eight-thirty.

"Rick. Wake up, Rick," she whispered, rubbing his shoulder as she had done every ten minutes for the past hour. "C'mon, Rick. If you get up now, you could still get to work by nine. Maybe he won't fire you."

He groaned and then turned to scowl at her. "Why don't you go find another job? I'll stay here with the kid."

"I...I don't think that would be good. You know how the baby's crying has been getting to you." She had come home one night to find Rick shaking their crying child in frustration. She quit her job the following morning.

Swinging her legs out from under the covers, she sat up. "C'mon. You can hop in the shower while I make you an egg sandwich to eat on the way."

Rick worked at the corner thrift store, but frequently hung over in the mornings—his period of sobriety long over—he hadn't been on time for over a week. What if he was fired? Or worse, what if he quit? She needed the time to pack her things—few that they were—to get things in order. It was over. She was finally ready to call it done.

"Just one more day, Lord," she prayed. "One more day and I'll leave. Really."

She turned and sighed in relief as Rick made himself sit up, rolling his head wearily. "I need coffee, angel face. Hot. And a lot of it."

"I'll make it right now." She swallowed hard. The thought of leaving was tougher when he was nice like that, calling her sweet names

instead of yelling at her or throwing things. It seemed every time she was ready to pack up and go, he could almost sense it and started to treat her better. But not today. She had to leave. It was time. For her. For Jared. For their future.

CHAPTER NINE

Eden arrived at Jared's door with a pail, a mop, rags, and a pounding heart. What was she doing? He answered her knock before she could turn tail and run.

"Eden!"

"Thought you might like some help," she said a bit sheepishly. "When you've been doing something as long as you have, it's bound to get tedious."

"You can say that again. Come in." He opened the door wider and stepped aside. "Can I get you anything? Water? Soda?"

"No, I'm fine. Just point me toward your present excavations, and I'll try and help."

"Great. I've cleared out those two walls already," he said, pointing toward the window wall and the one closest to the front door. "Now I'm working on this one," he said, moving toward the fireplace. The stacks on either side of the river-rock chimney reached his shoulders.

"Were the others as high?"

"Yes. So see? Haven't just been sitting here twiddling my thumbs."

"It's hardly a vacation."

"No. But it's been fun, too. Nick helps out on occasion, and we've found some really cool things." His expression grew distant.

"Jared?"

"Oh, sorry. Well, have a look for yourself." He led her over to the dining room table, covered with things she assumed they meant to keep. There was a large pile in the center of the room, made up mostly of newspapers and magazines, probably on its way to the dump.

"Wonderful," Eden mused, picking up a pair of snowshoes.

"I thought they'd look great over the mantel."

"They would. The old timers used to call them 'bear paws.'"

He smiled at her, and she set down the snowshoes and looked around some more. "A dance card," she mused. "Waltz, Quadrille, Lancers-Saratoga," she read.

"Sometimes I long for the days when people would get together as a community and do things like dancing."

"You dance?" she asked, trying to hide her interest.

"I hold my own. Look here," he said, lifting a deerskin pouch. "Bullets are still in it."

"To go with this," she said, touching the buttery soft fringe of a buckskin shirt. She glanced beyond it to a row of dark blue glass ink bottles, short and round, about the size of a baby food jar, with a narrow neck. "Did your uncle write a lot?"

"Not to me. Probably just another thing to collect."

There were old black-and-white photos that she sifted through. "Look at this," she directed, handing one to him. "That's the Going-to-the-Sun Highway." She came closer and pointed out the details. "When it was a dirt road. And with no guardrails!"

"Scary?" he asked.

"Very. You'll have to get up there soon. Take Nick. It's incredibly beautiful. And you'll be glad to see the rails when you find out how often you want to stare out across the valley and not at the road."

"I'll do that," he said. They got to work shortly thereafter. Jared asked her to set aside anything "interesting" and dump the rest. The majority of the pile was newsprint and magazines, some dated as old as 1952, none of which Jared cared to keep. They talked about the weather and the crowds in Bigfork as they worked.

"A lot of people come here in the summer and think they want to live here."

"What happens when they do?" Jared asked, resting his elbow on a pile of *Life* magazines.

"Many hit one Canadian-border winter and head home. It's gorgeous here in the summer, but you pay for it November through March. If you can't like both, you don't last long."

"Don't you get lonely on the lake, come winter?"

"I like the quiet, the solitude. As I said, you have to appreciate all the seasons to make the most out of them. Not much you can do about it anyway."

"Other than head to Arizona."

"Yes. That would resolve it. But you'd miss something important. Like the snowmelt and the spring buds. The flash of a blue jay's wing when spring still seems impossibly far away."

He stared at her for a moment, and she realized she was waxing on. She turned back to her stack.

"Eden, may I ask you something personal?"

"I guess." She braced herself.

"Have you ever been...involved? Married?"

"Close," she said with a hollow laugh. "I was in the gown and everything." She dared to look at Jared then. "Then my groom decided that he didn't love me after all."

"Ouch," he said with a wince. "That must've been brutal."

"Yes, it was." She kept working. "What about you? Nick tells me you've been divorced for a while."

"His mom and I divorced three years ago." He paused, but Eden dared not look up. "Three years. I was hoping we would get back together. Hoping somehow that I had just been an idiot in pushing for a divorce the last time Patricia saw other men while we were married. I don't know. I thought she had changed."

"And?"

"She hadn't. She won't. We apparently see marriage from different perspectives."

"Like?"

"She sees it as a security blanket but something she can toss aside in a moment. I see it as a sacred trust." He grinned at her ruefully. "The two don't exactly mesh."

"No, I can see why. So…you're not hoping to get back together any longer?"

"No." He turned back to his stack. "Buried that dream before I came here."

"Okay," Eden said, hearing that the tone of her voice was unnaturally bright. She softened it a bit. "I hope you guys have a great time."

"Eden, are you sure you're okay with this?" Jared asked over the phone line.

"Oh, fine, *fine*. It's not every day you get an invitation to take your son into the back country by horseback."

"Still, I feel bad canceling our fishing plans."

"Hey, it's still July. There's a lot of summer left. Unless you're heading back to New York tomorrow." She found that she was holding her breath.

"No. The office has started calling again, but I'm still keeping them at bay."

"Well, there you go. We have all kinds of time." But they didn't. And Eden didn't like the jolt of fear the idea sent through her heart. She had let Jared in, just a tiny bit. But it was clearly too far. Didn't today show her that? He was ready to toss her aside on a moment's notice.

"You're sure you're okay with it?"

"I'm fine, Jared. Really. Thanks for calling. Now go get your gear together and have a good time with Nick." *Go off to the Bob Marshall Wilderness. Without me. With that pretty cook who goes on all the trips and flirts with all the city-boys-turned-mountain-men.*

"Thanks for being such a sport, Eden. I'll catch you when I get home."

"Sure." *We'll see about that.* "'Bye." She hung up the heavy black phone and sat staring at it for a moment, then sighed. "It's high time I go in to see Gram anyway," she muttered. She suddenly felt claustrophobic in her little home, eager to get out. Eden rose from her stool at the counter and grabbed a sweater from the couch. It was a perfect day in the valley, but one never knew if a thunderstorm would whip up come late afternoon.

Eden walked through the clean, homey halls of Briarhurst, smiling at one resident, waving at another as she passed. It was here that she had allowed just one of her sculptures to be public—a lovely depiction of her grandmother's weathered form cradling a much younger Eden in her lap. It was so cheerful, so endearing, that the residents still hadn't stopped talking about it, not even three years after it had been installed in the central foyer of the senior residence. Only the joint power of her grandmother's stubborn insistence and the sorrow of not being able to care for Gram herself had persuaded Eden to allow it. It still made her uneasy as she passed; there was always an angle that bothered her, an edge that had needed more work.

"Hey, Gram," she said with a smile, turning a corner into her grandmother's open doorway. The old woman was sitting in a wheelchair by the large picture window, staring at a blue jay on the bird feeder. "Isn't he beautiful?" Eden exclaimed, coming closer to hug her.

"Oh, that old thing," Gram said in disgust, waving at him. "Sure he's pretty, but he scares off all the little ones!" She was indignant, always the champion of those who could not help themselves. In her younger years she had been a high-school principal and a pillar of the First Presbyterian Church of Kalispell—both jobs that utilized her underdog defender nature. "Come here again," she said, raising her thin arms for another hug. "What's been keeping you away?"

Eden smiled ruefully and sat down on the edge of her bed. "I'm sorry, Gram. Silly excuses."

"Let's hope it's a man. That biological clock of yours must be ticking."

"Haven't we given up on that?" Eden asked easily, shaking her head. Gram always said exactly what was on her mind, just as Renee and Sara did.

Gram narrowed her eyes at her. "No! Don't you worry about it anyway—I had your dad when I was forty. There's plenty of time."

"Yeah," she said, not sounding sure at all.

"Have something to tell me, child?"

"No," Eden said, wanting to throw her intuitive grandmother off her track. "I've just been busy."

"Oh," Gram said, clearly not believing her. "Yes."

"How have you been?"

"Won at bingo last night. The night before, bridge."

"You *shark*. The little old ladies have no chance against you."

"It's an even playing field, in my book. I'm just as old as any of them. Except for Mrs. Shubert. She must be ninety. Hasn't taken care of herself like I have. If I could still get out on the golf course, I'd show your brother a thing or two."

"Paul's not getting much golf in this summer," Eden said, thinking of her brother in Missoula. A forestry professor at the university, he had signed on to teach summer classes to earn some extra money. His wife, Susan, was expecting their new baby in October and had decided to stay at home for a while afterward.

"Did you bring me any candy?"

Eden laughed. "You're as bad as a kid. No, I didn't. But what do you say we get out of here for a while? Go for a drive, dinner? We could pick up some candy on the way back."

Gram clapped her hands together, and Eden stared at them, transfixed for a moment by their image. They would make a nice sculpture on their own. "That would be wonderful!" she was exclaiming. "I haven't been out of here for a month!"

Another pang of guilt shot through Eden. With her parents traveling the world and her brother busy in Missoula, almost three hours away, her grandmother was her responsibility. She should be looking in on Gram more often. For a while she had been coming once a week. But last year it had dropped to two times a month, and recently even less.

She got Gram ready and stopped at the front desk to tell the attendants they were going out for the evening. Then they climbed into Eden's truck and headed out of the parking lot.

"Where do you want to go?" Eden asked, leaning against the steering wheel.

"Why don't you head north on Stillwater Road? I'd like to see the old place."

The retirement home was but a half-mile from the farm where Gram had lived for years. She could even see the old red barn from her room. The farmlands were gradually receding into fields of suburban development, but at least this part of the valley was reserved for five-acre parcels and was still dominated by fields of wheat and alfalfa. They drove north, and Eden smiled as Gram painstakingly rolled her window down.

"Isn't that a bit too much?" she shouted over the wind.

Gram gave her a look that said *pshaw* and leaned back against the truck's seat, smiling as she closed her eyes. It was the smell of home—of ripening grain and dust and heat. Eden smiled, glad to be with her grandmother again, riding through lands that had for a hundred years sustained her family. To the west and north of the rich, verdant valley were lush, green mountains, to the east dominated the Continental Divide—marked by a towering range that watched over the valley below like granite sentinels. To the south, Flathead—the grandest freshwater lake west of the Mississippi—spread from mountain to mountain, ending thirty miles south in a rich marshland, home to a bird reserve. The more diminutive Swan Lake, eleven miles long, ran parallel to the grand lake, separated from the northernmost part of it by Crane Mountain. Their rivers met in Bigfork.

"Your great-great-grandfather homesteaded this land in 1882, before old Conrad ever thought about building a town called Kalispell."

Eden nodded her head, knowing the story by heart but enjoying it anew each time.

"His horses got away from him, some five miles south. He chased them all the way up here, crested that hill right there, and found himself in the middle of grasses that reached his waist. The horses weren't budging, but then neither was he. He was home."

Eden smiled, thinking of a young man in dungarees and suspenders, surveying the land, considering what his farm might look like someday. "Gramps was born on that farm, wasn't he?"

"Yes. My Frank was born in your great-grandmother's bedroom downstairs. Many were having their children in the hospital in town in those days, but your great-grandmother, she was a stubborn one. All five were born at home. Course, only three lived."

Eden nodded. As they whipped by the old farm, childhood memories—dropping stones down the three-hundred-foot well, picking green apples from the orchard, hiding in the dirty, decaying old barn—cascaded through her mind. The place had gone to a distant cousin some years back, the result of some tragic business deal in the sixties. Ernie and Martha had moved to the Swan River in 1960, soon after he had lost the farm, but the family had still gathered there for years afterward. Even as a child, Eden had picked up on the sense of melancholy about the old place off of Stillwater Road.

"Did Great-grampa Ernie ever get over losing it?"

"Never. He had poured his life into that place. Your Gramps and I, we would have worked it after them had he not lost it. As it was, we found our own way in the world, and it was probably for the best. Funny how it all works out."

"And it was Ernie who drowned in the river, right?"

"Yes. It was a beautiful summer day," she said, holding her hands up as if picturing it all over again. "We were planning on heading down to the river that day. Even your mama and daddy were with us. Paul was just a baby, and you weren't born yet. Grampa Ernie had gone out fishing, as he did every morning—Martha had a thing for trout for breakfast—and then she heard the most awful noise.

"By the time she got to the porch door, Ernie was swimming. Swimming! The man was over eighty, if he was a day. Headed toward that poor girl who was trapped in that old car. Martha could hear a baby crying and a woman screaming.

"And there was Ernie, trying to save the driver, God bless his soul. He got to the car and probably saw that the woman was trapped inside. He saved the baby though." Gram's expression was distant, distressed, as if seeing it in her mind. "Do you know that man got all the way to the river's edge without letting the baby go under again?"

Eden shook her head, although she had heard this story many times too. It still made her wonder. At her great-grandfather's bravery and the tragedy of the event.

"We lost Ernie that day. A young woman and an old man, dead. Oh, it was so sad! And there was your great-grandmother, crying over poor Ernie, holding that baby boy and wondering who on earth he belonged to."

"Who did he belong to? Someone on the river?"

"Why, he was Rudy Conway's grand-nephew. The baby's mother was his niece. Rudy was never the same after—"

"Wait. *Wait,*" Eden said, pulling the car to a stop. She stared at her grandmother. "That baby he saved was a relative of Rudy Conway's? They were heading to Rudy's?"

"Why, yes. I think I have that right."

Eden sat back, staring straight ahead at the gravel road that crested and disappeared a mile ahead of her. But she was doing the math. "That was about in the early sixties, right?"

"'61, I think."

"That would make him about thirty-nine. He said he was almost forty…"

"Who? Who are you talking about?"

Eden checked her rearview mirror and pulled back out onto the road. She shook her head. What were the chances? "I'm talking about Jared Conway, Gram. That baby Great-grampa saved from the river? He's back. And he's a full-grown man."

Jared and Nick borrowed bikes from the Sundquists one evening and went for a long ride, beginning with Jared's jogging route. They left the rush of the river and rode on the gravel road that led toward Bigfork, past hard-won fields carved from the pine forest and an old, gnarled apple tree Jared loved, complete with a ladder of a similar age leaning against it. They rode past farm outbuildings giving in to decomposition, dark gray wood returning to the black rich soil, and golden fields of hay. Jared breathed deeply, appreciating the warmth of the late-July evening, the perfection of the day.

It had been a good week. The five-day pack trip had been fabulous—he and Nick had really connected as they fished for trout that weighed as much as three pounds and photographed a mother grizzly and moose one day, elk and deer the next. They hiked to the top of three different peaks, able to see all the way into Canada. They ate by the fire and slept out underneath the stars, side by side.

"Doing okay, Nicolaus?" he called over his shoulder.

"Fine, Dad."

"Want to go a little farther?"

"If you do."

Jared smiled and led his son to a loop that took them back to the river over a forgotten logging road. They stopped at an abandoned cabin, probably more than a hundred years old, and poked around the interior.

"What do you think they were doing here?"

"Who knows," Jared said. "Maybe they were going to homestead, clear the land like those other folks did."

"That'd be hard."

"You're not kidding. Can you imagine pulling those old trees out of here? Not just cutting them down but getting rid of all the trunks and roots. Backbreaking, that's what it would be." Jared leaned against an old tamarack and looked up. Oddly, there was something appealing to the thought. The thought of physical, sweaty work. The kind that would make a man sit back at the end of the day, mindful of aching muscles from head to toe but able to say to his wife, "I cleared that back section today." That was the troublesome part of dealing in commodities. It was all on paper. He never lifted or pushed or felt the product in which he worked. He was five steps removed, a gambler of sorts. Jared shook his head. "Better get back. It's getting to be dinnertime."

"I think I hear the river."

"Yes. It isn't far. We'll come out by the lake, near the bridge."

"Want to stop and see Eden?"

The question took Jared by surprise. In the two days they had been home, he hadn't worked up the nerve to go see her. Truth be told, he didn't know if he wanted to see her. He had called a couple of times but then found himself relieved when she didn't answer. *You're all mixed up, Jared Conway. You better get it straight before you jump into something you aren't prepared to handle.*

"Sure. If you do."

When they reached the lake, and then a clearing where they could see Eden's house, Jared swallowed his disappointment that she was not in view. Somehow he had hoped she would be on the porch working or in the garden that was surrounded by an eight-foot deer fence. "Maybe she's not home."

"Maybe. We could go see."

"Yes, we could."

"Dad?"

"Yeah?"

"Are you falling in love with Eden?"

"I don't know, Nick. Maybe. Is that hard for you to imagine?"

"No," the boy said slowly. "And yes. Does that mean you and Mom aren't getting back together?"

Jared reached out and held Nick's shoulder. "Nicolaus, no matter what happens with Eden, your mom and I are never getting back together."

The child sighed and stared at the dirt road. "You're not even going to try again?"

"No. We're not going to try again. I'm sorry, Son. I know that's what you wanted. It just…it just isn't going to work."

The boy nodded sagely, like an old priest hearing confession. "It's okay, Dad. I know you tried."

"Thanks, Nick."

Nicholas pulled his head over one shoulder, toward Eden's. "Let's go see if Eden's home. Race ya," Nick said, already ahead.

Jared smiled and pedaled hard after him.

When they reached her porch, they could see her sitting out on the dock, staring down the lake, looking lovely in a buttery sundress that she had pulled up to her knees in order to dangle her tanned legs in the cool water, obviously combating the heat of the evening.

"Dad, let's surprise her! Let's go jump in!" Nicolaus whispered.

The water looked inviting, and Jared smiled. "Okay. But don't get her wet."

They ran down the grassy embankment, tearing their shirts off, whooping and hollering in glee. Nick ran to the end of the dock, waved at Eden as only a goofy eight-year-old could do, then dived in. Jared paused beside her. "Do you mind?"

"Not at all."

Jared dove in, appreciating the cleansing, exhilarating rush of the cool water after their long, hot, dusty ride. Nick swam for shore and paused to search the shallows for treasure. Jared swam to the dock and rested his forearms on the end, kicking to stay upright. "Going somewhere?" he asked lightly, gesturing toward her dress. Then before she could say anything, he said, "You didn't answer your phone."

"Yes and no, to your questions. I decided I wouldn't today."

"Any reason?"

"No," she said, cocking her head, still looking down the lake. "I think I just wanted to be left alone." She glanced at him then, and Jared was startled by how pretty she looked.

"Oh. Want us to go?"

"No. That's okay. I'm leaving in a minute to go to the play," she said with a gentle smile.

"Ah. Theatre even in Bigfork, Montana, huh?"

"You can kill the 'ain't Broadway' speech. They're quite good. They audition players from around the country. Up-and-comers."

He pulled himself up and shook his head to dry off somewhat. When she raised her hands and ducked, he said, "Oh! Sorry!"

"It's all right. Just sit before you do any more damage."

Jared sat down beside her and dangled his legs in the water too. It was so clear, he could see to the green bottom, twelve feet down. Giant squawfish canvassed the rocks, searching for supper, even as a small school of minnows flitted under the dock. Nick waded out of the lake and headed toward the boathouse, apparently to poke around. "Do you know where the old bridge was?" Jared asked.

She looked at him strangely, her smile fading, as if she knew the truth about what had happened there. But she couldn't know. Could she?

"It was downriver. Just south of my great-grandparents' cabin."

"Near ours?"

"Just around the bend."

"Did you ever see it?"

"No. I wasn't born yet. By the time I was around, the new bridge was in place up here."

Something in her tone made him feel as if she did indeed know, that she knew him in a more intimate way than any other. How could that be? He stared at her, communicating without speaking, wondering at her beauty in the warm light of a hot summer evening. The shadows caught the hollow of her cheekbones, the narrow bridge of her nose, illuminated her wide, dark eyes. The sun on the dappling water reflected on her face and dress. He resisted the urge to lean over and kiss her. Slowly he reached up and ran the back of his fingers across her rounded cheek and then traced a finger across her bowed lips, finding himself frowning in his intensity.

"I've got to go," she whispered, not moving at all. She was so good, so pure. So beautiful. Funny how he hadn't seen it before. He'd noticed it a little at her prayer spot and again in town, with other little glimpses here and there. But she was. She was lovely.

"I hope you enjoy it," he said softly. They stared at each other a moment longer. He tore his eyes from hers and looked for his son. "Nick, don't fool with that!" Nicolaus was at her canoe, turning it over.

"It's all right," she said, placing a calming hand on his forearm. Her touch was strangely comforting, healing. She rose and slipped on delicate white sandals over her damp, sun-browned feet. Jared followed her off the dock and up the hill to see her off. "Come on, Nick," he called.

Eden came out of the house with her purse and keys. "Did you have a good time in the mountains, Nick?"

"The best! You should've seen the rainbows we landed, Eden! I just did that potato thing, and there they were, one after another!"

"I know. Isn't it great? I haven't been to the Bob Marshall Wilderness in years, but I love it every time I go."

"Where're you going?" Nick asked.

"To see a musical. In Bigfork. *Anything Goes.*"

Jared followed her to the old truck, with Nick trailing behind, then opened the door for her. She pulled it shut firmly after she got in.

"Good night, gentlemen," she said, gently smiling through the window. "Thanks for the visit. You're welcome to make yourselves at home on the porch or go for a canoe ride if you want to spend some time on the lake."

"Thanks. Good night, Eden."

Jared watched as the truck went out the driveway and disappeared down the tree-lined road. He stared until the image of her in that buttery dress faded a little.

"Want to go sit on her dock?" Nick asked.

"Sure." They walked back out onto the dock, and Jared stared down through the crystalline waters to the rocks of aubergine, turquoise, cobalt, and clay. What did he want from this place? Why had he not just finished emptying the cabin and signed the papers with Julie Vose to sell it? Patricia had begun calling again, demanding that he bring their son home. Somehow a two-week vacation had folded into six, going on seven, and he had no desire to return. When Don hassled him about coming back to work, Jared had reminded him that he had accrued sixty days of vacation over the years. What was going on inside him? What did he need? Where was he going? What was he doing? He wanted something, something definitive, something that would guide his course as he made the choices that would determine the second act of his life. He didn't want to make any more mistakes, which were inevitable, he knew, but he could try, couldn't he? He wanted to become grounded, settled like Eden. Grounded and yet free.

All he knew for sure was that the taste of peace and happiness he had found here in the Swan Valley had left him thirsty for more.

"You miss home, Nick?"

"Not really."

"Me neither. So you're not ready to head back?"

Nick looked at him in alarm. "We were just there! Can't we stay here? For the rest of the summer?"

Jared laughed under his breath. "I don't know if it can be that long." He reached up and put an arm around his son. "But at least a little longer. Your mom's missing you."

"She should come here."

Jared smiled again. "I don't think this would be fun for your mother."

"Why not?"

"She's always been more a fan of Macy's than Montana. She's a city person."

"Are you a country person?"

"Getting more that way, it seems. Getting more that way."

"You can't take my car!" he shouted.

"It's mine just as much as yours," she mumbled, tucking her baby boy into the bassinet in the front seat of the Buick. Sound asleep, Jared looked like a perfect cherub.

"I won't let you," he said, coming close. "Give me the keys, Anna." His brow furrowing, his eyes menacing, he gripped her forearm and shook it, as if to shake the keys loose.

"Rick, I'm leaving." She pulled her arm away. If she showed any weakness, she knew it would be all over. Rick would win.

"He's my son! That's my car!"

"He's my son now, Rick. You had your chance to be his father, give him your name. But you didn't want to do that. And it's more my car than yours—I've made most of the payments." She took a breath. "I need to go away, pull myself together. Make some plans. You and I aren't…working." She swallowed hard, reached up to caress his strong jaw line one last time. He swatted her hand away. "Good-bye, Rick. I'll write when we get there."

"You haven't even told me where you're going." His tone had changed from fury to fear as he stared at her through the driver's-side window.

She looked into his deep brown eyes one last time. "That's right." Anna turned the key, gunned the engine, and quickly pulled out onto the highway, never looking back.

CHAPTER TEN

That following Sunday, Eden did a double take when she saw Jared and Nick enter the small church in Ferndale, a tiny community a few miles from Bigfork. She nudged her brother, up from Missoula for a weekend visit, to move down the pew and make room, then looked back up at Jared. "I didn't know you attended church," she said in a low voice.

"It's been awhile," he said with a half-shrug. "Thought it was time again."

Eden nodded as if he weren't saying anything odd at all. She wondered if it was happenstance that had led them to the tiny, white-clapboard chapel she had come to call hers or if it was just the closest to them, on the highway en route to Bigfork. She smiled to herself. If it had been awhile since Jared had come to church, he was in for a treat. The congregation was small in number but mighty in spirit.

Paul elbowed her, obviously awaiting an introduction. "Jared, this is my brother, Paul. He's visiting me this weekend from Missoula. Paul, this is Jared and Nick. They're staying on the river."

Jared smiled and gave her brother's hand a firm shake in front of Eden, while Nick gave him a little wave. Paul leaned back, but not before he had given his sister a meaningful glance, as if to say, *You didn't tell me about him.*

As if there was anything to tell.

They rose with the congregation, singing the opening hymn, "Great Is Thy Faithfulness." At the hymn's conclusion, the young woman at the piano segued beautifully into another, "Beautiful Savior." Eden dared to steal a glance at Jared. He was singing, singing as loudly as if he had been in church all his life.

Suddenly Eden found herself praying for Jared. She prayed that he would find direction. She prayed that he would find peace. She prayed that he would find God.

At the last second she elected not to pray for *them*. As a couple. After all, there really wasn't anything that led her to believe there could be a "them" anyway. First it had to be about Jared. Then maybe, just maybe, it could be about Jared and Eden.

If she wanted that at all.

Jared enjoyed the service far more than he had expected. The pastor had been sincere but low-key. Interesting but not dominating. Like a wise old fishing buddy one could turn to for advice or direction. The image appealed to Jared. Even Nick had done okay, fidgeting only for the last half-hour of singing and praying. "Praise time" the pastor had called it.

The congregation had moved out of the little church en masse, eager to catch a breath of air as the August morning gave way to high-noon heat. Nick ran for the playground, and Jared had to bob and weave to see where he went. There was a boy about his age there already, and soon Michael Sundquist joined them. It was Michael who had convinced Nick to give the church a try. That was how they had ended up at the tiny church in Ferndale. Seeing Eden was a welcome surprise.

"So, you're staying on the river?" Paul Powell asked, suddenly at his side.

"Yeah. Been there for almost two months. I inherited my Uncle Rudy's cabin. We came to clean it out and sell it but ended up staying."

Paul nodded, studying him as he would an adversary as much as a potential friend. *Big brother,* Jared assessed. He found himself standing up a little straighter.

"Rudy's place, huh?" Paul commented. "It must've been a mess."

"You could say that," Jared said, smiling. "It's getting better. Lot of junk to get rid of but a few treasures, too."

"I can imagine."

"So, you're here for a visit?" He listened for Paul's response, but his eyes were drawn to Eden, walking up to them. Dressed in a rose-colored linen jumper and a button-down, white cotton blouse, she managed to look fresh even in the hot, dry heat.

"Just overnight," Paul said slowly, following his gaze. "How long you think you'll stay on the river?"

"Haven't decided. I'd like to stay until September, but my ex-wife has been calling a lot lately. She wants to see our son too."

"Must be tough, being a divorced dad."

"Sometimes. Mostly I'm just happy to be a dad."

"Know what you mean. Got a third on the way."

"Congratulations! That's gotta be exciting."

"Only the best. I'm sure you remember."

But it was hard for Jared to remember those months years

ago. Patricia had been sick all nine months of her pregnancy, and he had been in the developmental stage of his business, working ninety-hour weeks. Jared recalled the stress of caring for an ailing wife, the burden of feeling he was the cause of her illness. No excitement, no joy. She had not allowed it, instead making him pay every day until Nick was born. Only the thrill of seeing his new son's slick, tiny, dark-haired scalp and hearing his first wail had made it okay—that was all he could remember of "excitement." It had made all the preceding months disappear. He had a son. *A son.* And he was only just now rediscovering that joy, eight years later.

"So, what are you and Nick up to today?" Paul was asking.

Jared jumped back to the present. "Not much. Thought we'd get some lunch, then head back to the cabin to do some more work."

"That doesn't sound like fun," Paul chided. "Why don't you come to Eden's?"

"Paul…" Eden said in a voice that said he presumed too much.

"What? It's okay, isn't it, Eden?"

"No, that's all right," Jared said quickly. "Thanks anyway. You two probably want to visit just as a family. We'll catch you some other time, Paul."

"Jared, no," Eden said. "I'm sorry. His invitation just surprised me, that's all. Come on over. We'll hang out on the dock and do something on the barbecue tonight. Paul and I will go have lunch together now and catch up. You guys can come later."

"I don't know."

"Come on," she said, smiling. "We'll borrow the Bakers' boat. Do some skiing."

He cringed. It had taken a week to get over the soreness the last time he skied, the day they got Nicolaus up for the first time. "How about just a boat ride?"

"We could take Nick down to the cliffs," Paul said.

"He'd like that," Eden said.

"The cliffs?"

"The old rock house on the other end of Swan. It's built on a cliff, and in the cove beside it, you can jump off—a fifteen-foot drop."

"Nick would love it," Jared said, wanting to accept but not wanting to push Eden.

"Come," she said once more.

That was all it took.

"So tell me about Jared Conway," Paul said, passing her the cheese plate. They were sitting on the porch, chatting and eating raspberries from her garden, fresh-baked bread, and Swiss cheese.

"Oh, I would much rather talk about you and the family," she said, biting into the yeasty white bread covered in butter.

"I bet you would. Come on. Spill it, little sister. There hasn't been a man in your life since what's-his-name left you on your wedding day. Susan would kill me if I came home with less than the entire story."

"You know about as much as I do. He's here with his son, staying in Rudy's cabin. Rudy died last year, did you know?"

"No, I hadn't heard that," he said, sorrow evident in his tone.

"Apparently he left the place to Jared. He came just to clean out the place and spend a little time with his son, and he got the Swan fever."

"Can hardly blame him," Paul said, gesturing to the lake and to her.

She shook her head. "Don't think it's me that's keeping him here. It's something else. I think it's his memories of his mother he's here to deal with. And Great-grampa Ernie." She paused, waiting for her words to sink in.

"What?"

"Jared Conway was the baby Ernie pulled out of the car—at the bridge."

"No way!"

"Yes."

"Is that how you two connected?"

"No. He doesn't even seem to know Ernie was our great-grandfather. Although I would bet he'll figure it out soon."

"Why don't you tell him?"

"There's just never a good time to say, 'Hey, did you know that it was my great-grandfather that saved your life?' Plus, I just found out from Gram myself."

"So how did you two meet?"

"I saved his son from a near catastrophe. Nick had waders on, went over the side of their boat and into a whirlpool current. I was fishing from the bank nearby, so I dove in and pulled them off before he drowned."

"Whoa," Paul said, sitting back and staring at her. "Weird kind of full-circle thing going on between you two, isn't there?"

"You could say that. I vacillate between thinking he could be the one—you know, the way he looks at me once in a while—and then feeling like I should hike up into the Bob and not come down until he leaves. It scares me. *He* scares me."

"I haven't seen a man look at you like that in ages."

"Well, thanks very much."

"No, really. I've seen guys look at you, appreciate you, but there's something different about Jared."

"Yeah, well, I don't know if anything could happen anyway. He's divorced and had just been trying to get back together with his wife. He's got issues."

"Who doesn't?"

"I mean *issues*."

"Don't let it scare you. Don't make yourself totally vulnerable in this, Eden—be smart—but don't close yourself off. Maybe he's on the brink of resolving all those issues."

"Maybe. You check him out this afternoon. See what you think."

"Happy to do so, little sis."

"Come on, Jared," Paul urged, scrambling up the cliff to the top.

It was high, much higher from on top than it looked from the boat. Jared told himself it was only a twelve- or fifteen-foot drop, nothing more than a high dive. But his heart was pounding. "Hold up, Nick," he warned. "Wait for me."

"Hurry up, man," Paul said. "Your boy's itching to go. Wish my girls were here," he called down to Eden, who sat in the boat to watch.

"You would just be pressuring them to jump, and they would be up there crying," she called back.

Jared could see why. He reached the top and stood, bare feet finding purchase on the hard, sharp edges of the cliff rock. He squared his shoulders and came alongside Nick and Paul. Below the emerald green waters waved, impossibly deep. Jared gripped the shoulder straps of his life vest and grimaced. What if the vest came off? What if he plunged down into the water with nothing to brake his descent? What if he didn't take a deep enough breath? What if the water sealed over him and didn't let him rise?

Paul had told him there was a train engine in the depths of this end of the lake—an old logging train that had gone through the ice and sunk from view within seconds. Had anyone been inside? Had another life been taken by these chilly mountain waters?

"High, huh?" Paul acknowledged. "But it's great. You'll love it when you're down."

"You go first, Dad."

"Sure. Sure," Jared repeated, stepping closer to the edge. He was being foolish; he needed to focus on something else besides the deep. He looked down. Directly below was a rock ledge that edged out from the cliff, just beneath the water. "No danger we'll hit that shelf?"

"No problem," Paul assured them. "Just be sure to step away from the cliff. It already pokes out a bit."

The wind picked up, making Jared shiver all the more.

"Go on, Dad."

"I'm goin'," he growled. His heart was pounding. This was idiotic. It was hard for him to catch his breath.

"You okay, man?" Paul asked. "Your color just went from healthy to dead."

"Fine." He looked across the lake, at the highway that ran along its edge. And with that he made himself step away from the cliff. Away from safety and sanity. He fought the crazy urge to turn and

grab the rock again, to try and stop his descent. The water came up
fast, and Jared plunged beneath the surface, already longing for air.
Fortunately the life vest did its work, and he popped up right away.
Paul was launching himself from the cliff with a whoop before Jared
could take his first breath.

"Wait!" he gasped, waving at Nick. "Don't!" But Nick didn't
seem to hear him. He just waved back.

"Jared? What's wrong?" Eden asked, rising from the boat to lean
over the back, toward him. "Are you all right?"

"Bombs away!" Nick called, gleefully parting from the cliff. He
seemed to hang in the air for several long seconds before entering the
water with a big splash. He popped up immediately and grinned
from ear to ear. "Cool! That was awesome! Let's do it again!"

"*No!* No, I think that's enough," Jared said, shaking his head.

"A young man's sport, eh?" Paul teased him. He climbed up the
ladder on the back of the boat and jumped inside.

Shaking, Jared waited until Nick was safely inside and then followed suit.

"Are you all right, Jared?" Eden asked in concern. She handed
him a beach towel. "You're shaking."

"It's cold," he covered. "Cold, that's all."

"But you told Nick to wait—"

"I just wanted to catch my breath. To catch my breath so I could
watch him."

"Oh," she said slowly.

"Let's head home!" Paul called over his shoulder. He sat down in
the driver's seat. "I'm starving."

"It's just you and me," Anna sobbed, trying to wipe her eyes so she could see the highway. She reached over and touched Jared, wanting the reassurance of his soft, warm skin as she considered the forever absence of Rick.

She was leaving him behind. And no, he hadn't been the best father, never a husband to her, but he had been something to her. Her first love, her only love. Her only family, really.

Jared cooed and smiled, as if Anna were making faces to coax a laugh. She laughed in spite of herself, through her tears.

"It will be okay," she said, still crying. "Mama's going to make it all okay. You'll like Montana. And Uncle Rudy. Uncle Rudy loves babies."

But her mind wasn't on Uncle Rudy. It was on the love she was leaving behind. Rick had been mean, yes. But he had been hers, and she had been his. And that belonging to someone was the sweetest, most treasured thing she had ever experienced. Away from him she felt like she may as well have been alone on the moon, tiny and lost.

"Keep us safe, Lord," she whispered, blinking and trying to find her focus on the road. "Get us home."

CHAPTER ELEVEN

"I like your brother," Jared said, joining Eden in the kitchen later that day.

"He likes you too."

"How often do you see each other?"

"Not often. Used to be more, but he's picked up extra hours at the university. Baby on the way and all."

"He's a good man." He leaned over the counter, watching her move from the fridge to the counter. She could feel his eyes on her.

"Yes, he is."

"What are you making?"

"Jezebel sauce. For the pork roast."

"Jezebel sauce? What's a good Christian girl like you doing making Jezebel sauce?" he teased.

"Devil shouldn't have all the fun," she quipped.

"No, that hardly would be fair," he said with a smile. "What's in it?" he asked, nodding at her bowl.

"Family secret. You can serve it over cream cheese as an hors d'oeuvre, on chicken, or in this case, pork." She leaned down and inhaled deeply. "Mmm. Here, smell." She lifted the bowl, and Jared took a big whiff.

He coughed, and his eyes began to tear up. "Good grief, woman! You trying to kill me?"

168 | Lisa Tawn Bergren

She giggled, and he saw he had been set up. "There's a healthy amount of mustard and horseradish in the sauce. You gotta be careful." She turned to baste the pork roast, then carried it out to the barbecue. Paul and Nick were still out on the water, giving the boy a run on the inner tube behind the Bakers' boat.

"I'll want to fill up the boat's gas tank," Jared said, looking out to where Paul was driving the boat in a slow circle, making huge waves for Nicolaus to jump. He shook his head, seemingly lost in the moment. "This place has been terrific for Nick."

Eden walked up alongside and stared out to the water with him. "It has? How 'bout for you?"

He stared at her then, intense. "For me, too."

She nodded and looked away. "I had better get this on, or we'll never eat."

Jared followed close behind. After a beat he said, "Nick will sure be hungry when he gets back. Your brother is a sport to take him out for so long."

"Are you kidding? He loves it. His daughters are pretty much girly-girls. No water skiing or inner-tubing for them. Once in a while we can talk them into a pull in the raft, going about two miles per hour."

"I bet you miss seeing them."

"I do. And they're just a couple of hours away! Somehow this summer has just raced by. I don't know what's been keeping me from getting them up here." She looked at him, then quickly away. She wasn't being honest. It was Jared who had occupied her mind and thoughts for weeks now. By this time last summer, she had had her nieces up for two weekends. This year she'd ignored them as badly as she had ignored Gram. For what? For a man who would leave any day? She was a fool. A fool for letting herself go as she had, for dreaming of the impossible.

"Eden." Jared let his warm, broad hand rest on her shoulder.

She jerked her head up from the barbecue and gently edged away.

"What are you thinking about?"

"Nothing."

"Well, you're just about killing that poor pig again with that sauce."

"Oh," she said, trying to cover her embarrassment. "I didn't notice. Could you do me a favor and go grab the salt and pepper?"

"Sure," he said slowly. He left her side, and she breathed a sigh of relief. Having him near her just about drove her crazy. One moment he was looking at her as though he wanted to spend the rest of his life with her, and the next moment he seemed two thousand miles away, thinking about his job or his ex-wife or something else, something deeper he had not shared with her. She wondered if it was the river and the mother who had died there that occupied so many of his thoughts. She wondered if she should tell him what she knew. But it was never the right time.

"It's almost time for the moonrise," Paul said, ducking his head in the kitchen window from the porch. Eden was elbow deep in dish soapsuds, and Jared was drying their supper plates. Washing dishes together had felt oddly intimate to Eden, and she felt saddened that it was over. "Nick and I brought the chairs out to the dock."

"We're coming," Eden said, smiling as Jared looked back and forth between them.

"Moonrise?"

"It's incredible. Here, take this cocoa to Nick and this coffee to my brother. I'll bring ours down in a second."

"Okay." He obediently took the mugs from the counter and headed down to the dock in the dark. Eden grabbed a thick sweat-shirt and followed behind. After the heat of the day, the mountain evening—especially out on the water—could be chilly. But as she walked down the stairs, she realized it was one of perhaps seven tem-perate summer nights of the year. Reaching the dock, she noted that the only available seat was right next to Jared. He moved over a bit, as if sensing her discomfort.

"There, see?" Paul asked. Down the lake, peeking over a ridge of silhouetted pines was the upper curve of a full moon. It was huge on the horizon, heavy, as if struggling in its climb. But it continued its ascent, rising, rising as they watched until it cleared the tree line.

The four of them observed it in silence until Nick broke their reverie with a "wow." They all laughed softly. The oily black water before them was mostly quiet, leaving the moon's reflection as a wavering, white circle. As they watched, a slight breeze blew down the lake, shattering the circle into a shimmering path that led from the dock to its originator on the horizon. The air was warm, though, and felt like the breath of God directly on her face.

"Incredible," Jared said, his voice barely audible.

Eden glanced at him, his face deeply shadowed and tilted upward at the moon before them.

"This place, this lake, this river, these mountains…they seem to speak to me again and again."

"What do they tell you?" Eden asked slowly, carefully.

"It's nothing spelled out. It's just kind of an overarching healing presence I feel here," he said.

"There's something about the valley that always makes it easier for me to pray, to meditate," Paul said. "When I'm out canoeing or hiking…it's as if God is more present here than any other place."

"Or maybe it's that you're more present here than any other place," Eden said, thinking of his crazy, busy life in Missoula.

"That, too," he agreed.

"Maybe that's what it is for me, too," Jared said. He turned toward Paul. "When you say you meditate here, do you mean meditate in the 'Om' tradition?"

Paul smiled, his white teeth gleaming in the dim light. "No. It's more like finding a quiet place and listening—talking to God, then waiting on him to speak."

Jared glanced at Eden as he associated Paul's words with seeing her at her praying spot. It was obviously there that she felt closest to her Lord, there that she could let down her guard and let God in.

"I think it's that we're surrounded by his incredible creation here, not by what man has built," Eden put in. "Sure, there are the multimillion-dollar homes and boats and all, but it's easier to see past it, to what God saw when he made it. We can put the things that distract us aside and simply listen for him, pay attention to how he's been present all through our day and week and month."

"Can I get more hot chocolate?" Nick whispered, obviously bored with the lofty talk of the adults.

"Sure," Jared and Eden said at the same time, then laughed a bit uneasily. The boy trotted down the dock and up toward the house.

"Do you think this place is healing?" Jared asked.

"It can be," Eden said.

"I think so," Paul added. "Maybe because I don't live here, I can see it better. But I swear God is more present here—or maybe Eden's right, maybe I'm just more aware here—but where God is, so is healing."

"Do you need healing?" Eden dared to ask Jared softly.

Jared paused for a moment, staring at his coffee mug. "My life's course really started here. And somehow," he looked over Eden's shoulder, up to the cabin where his son could be seen in the kitchen window, "somehow I took some bad turns. Made some wrong choices. Nick is the best thing that ever happened to me, but his mother and I—we thought of marriage in different terms. I own my own business, and it's doing great, but lately I find myself just not caring if I go back at all. I've always loved New York, but being here, I've discovered a whole new way of living. I find myself dreading the return to my old life. It feels distant, impersonal, unimportant."

He turned to her. "So maybe that's where I need healing. I need new vision, new encouragement to make the best of what I have there."

"Or maybe you need healing for where you feel your 'life course' took the wrong turn."

He stared at her for a long moment, as if trying to see her better in the moonlight, to discern what her words meant. "I was so young. The choices that were made here for me were not mine to make."

"Which doesn't make them easier to handle."

"No."

"What are you referring to?" Paul asked. "If it's not too personal..."

"There was an accident. My mother died on the old bridge, and I was saved."

Paul was quiet for a second, then said, "You were the baby who was saved. You, Jared Conway, were somewhat famous in these parts as we grew up. We often wondered what happened to you."

"You knew about the accident? You knew about me?"

"Everyone knew about you," he said calmly. "We forgot your name, that Rudy was your family, but you became a local legend." Paul stared over the rim of his mug at the lake ahead. "A man starts his life like that," he allowed, "he's bound to have to deal with something down the road."

"I guess that's why I'm here," Jared said. "I guess that's what God wants me to do. I'm just now figuring out why my mother was bringing me here and dealing with the sacrifices she made for me. It's a lot to take in, you know? Knowing that you were saved but your mother wasn't? I feel as if my life should be worth more, that I should be living a life worthy of two."

Eden met Paul's gaze and shook her head slightly. She knew they were both thinking of their great-grandfather and the sacrifice he made. But Jared had to come to terms with his mother—and God—before he could take on a stranger. Especially when that stranger was the kin of Eden Powell. She felt soul-sure of it.

"Then there was the old man," he continued. "You guys would know. Who was the old man who pulled me out? My aunt and uncle told me he died—"

"Jared," Eden interrupted, praying for divine guidance. "You said you felt as if you should live for two. Three, really, if you count the old man. But sacrifices are often gifts from another. And sometimes gifts cannot be repaid. The only way to honor the gift is to accept them, appreciate them, be thankful for them."

"But we're talking about *lives* lost, Eden." His voice was filled with pain.

"Yes, I know. The only one who has ever done that for me was Christ. When I consider his sacrifice, how he would've died and only for me, it demonstrates how greatly—how deeply—I am loved. It moves me to act in ways that honor him. It reminds me that no matter how far I wander, he is there, ready to hold out his hand if I will just come home." Eden shivered, feeling the Spirit move through her words. "That, Jared, is what sacrifice is about. It is love beyond the years. Your mother, your God, the old man who pulled you out, would want nothing more than for you to find peace and love in your life."

Jared listened as if the words were penetrating his soul. "Healing. That's what you're talking about. Finding the path to live your life to the fullest."

"Healing…peace…love…*life*. It's all about the *bridge*. Jesus is the bridge between our distant, chaotic, stubbornly sinful lives and healing. Don't you see, Jared? He's the bridge. And everyone must cross a bridge before healing and peace and forgiveness and love can find them."

Eden had gone with Renee to an art show in Great Falls and was not due back for a couple of days. Jared found himself missing her, and he ran by her place, ostensibly to "check on things" but mostly to sit and think, about her, about her words to him on the dock that night of the moonrise. He ambled around her cottage that mid-August morning, jumping off the porch, leaning one arm against a towering ponderosa pine with its puzzle-like bark, and staring out to a busy lake full of "summer people," as she called them. He looked back to the towering, centuries-old tree, with its red-tone covering split by huge rivulets of black, like battle scars on a veteran. Here and there, pitch cascaded downward in small frozen waterfalls that resembled dried honey.

Jared picked off a piece of foamy bark and broke it into tiny pieces, watching as they fell to the fading summer grass at his feet. Having her gone made Jared feel unsettled, antsy, and he hadn't slept well in days. What was going on? When had he begun falling a little in love with her?

He threw the last of the bark to the ground and ran up the hill, past the cottage, toward the road above. The creak of an open door made him pause, and he turned to see the door of the storage building swinging back and forth in the breeze. Frowning, he walked over to the tiny shed and peered in, making sure things were in order. Jared was shutting the door when he caught sight of the figure on the ground, huddled beneath a sheet of plastic. He did a double take, thinking at first that it was a person, then laughed at himself. It was only a sculpture. Cocking his head, he left the door ajar and felt for the light switch. Unsuccessful, he cast for a pull cord and found it at last. A bare bulb lit up the dim room.

He crouched and studied the sad, frightened woman cowering under one hand, searching with another. He pulled back the plastic and ran his hand along the lines of her back, careful not to damage the white-fired form but wanting to feel something that Eden had created. It was eerie how she had caught the terror and trembling of the woman. What had scared her so? What was within Eden that she could convey such emotion in clay? He marveled at her for a moment, bending low to see the figure from a different angle, then hurrying to cover her with the plastic, feeling as if he were intruding on Eden as surely as that day he had stumbled upon her by the river. And yet he was just as transfixed. He stood, intending to go, but could not take his eyes from the woman. How had Eden done this? Why had she not shared her talent with the world? It struck him then. Maybe the figure was her, cowering beneath her own fears even as she sought to reach out, to venture forward.

Jared turned and pulled the cord on the light, resolutely closing the door behind him and making sure it was latched. But he left his hand on the handle for a moment, the figure still vivid in his mind. Then he turned to run up her driveway to the road beyond. As much as he knew that statue held some key to Eden's inner fears, he felt a connection to those troubled emotions within himself. Lately it was only getting worse. He ran faster and faster, as fast as he could, trying to escape the demons of his past while still ducking the fears his future brought near.

He would have to leave soon. Buckley was scheduled to resume classes at the end of the following week—he had already asked for permission to bring Nick back late, but he was just putting off the inevitable. His partner, Don, was on the verge of calling in psychiatric help for Jared, so convinced was he that the man had gone off the deep end. And Patricia was threatening legal action if he didn't bring their son "home" soon. *Suddenly the doting mother,* he thought, slowing to angrily kick a stone into the woods. Still, he knew Nick missed her. And he was being unfair; Patricia hadn't betrayed their son, only him. She wasn't a bad mother, just better at it when it came in short-term spurts. Like in marriage, over the long haul she wearied of her role.

He picked up his pace again and found himself on the deer trail that led to Eden's prayer spot. He slowed and stopped, leaning over to pant and consider. Did he really want to go there? Did he really want to encounter what she and Paul seemed to experience so freely? He turned to head back to the bridge, to go home, then turned again, walking slowly toward the cottonwood grove, feeling his pulse rate slow to normal.

It was a cool morning. There were high clouds rolling in, bent on destroying the afternoon plans of the vacationers on the lake, no doubt. The breeze rustled through the leaves high overhead and then those closer to him, the birch leaves beginning to show the tinge of autumn's yellow promise. He ducked and bent and made his way to the trampled grasses of Eden's prayer spot. There he sat down, leaning against an adolescent birch with his knees bent before him. He sat there for a while relaxing, smelling the peat moss clinging to rocks that were soaking up all the sun's heat they could and the fresh, water-heavy odor of the river beneath him. He closed his eyes, listening to the gusts as they moved through the grove, then beyond to the pines. Then he let go of all that troubled him, one thought at a time, until he felt nearly depleted. He listened and waited. For Eden and Paul's God to draw near. For *his* God.

But all he heard were the sounds of the forest.

Anna hadn't eaten in three days, and her milk was running dry. The sense of helplessness consumed her. Still eight hundred miles from northwest Montana, she stopped at a small-town market and counted her cash again, hoping against hope that it would somehow expand. She shook her head. It would take all she had to get to her uncle's. If not more. And she still needed to wash a load of diapers. The baby was getting a terrible rash from staying too long in wet ones. She gazed down at him and shifted the boy in her arms, watching as he again latched on to her breast, obviously frantic to find the right position to get the milk flowing.

Anna swallowed hard through her tears. She had to buy a quart of milk and some bread. For her, to get her own milk flowing, and for the baby right now. If her milk was gone for good, they were in serious trouble. He was wailing now, angry that he was hungry and not appeased. It was cold in the car, but it was too expensive for Anna to warm it up by running the engine. They had to conserve.

A sudden knock on her window scared her, making her gasp, and Jared wailed more loudly.

There was a kindly looking woman outside, so Anna rolled down the window. "Do you need some help, miss? Are you all by yourself?" the lady asked.

"No, I'm fine," Anna said, trying to wipe away her tears. "I'm just...I'm just..."

"Trying to feed your baby?" the woman supplied helpfully. "It's hard on the road. I fed my own—my youngest—on the road, when we were moving out west." She nodded toward a Silver Streak camper parked on the side of the lot. "Sometimes it's better if you can get warm, have a little room. My husband and I were just sitting down to some supper. We have a little extra. Why don't you come over and share a meal with us, get warm, and give me a turn with that child? Had seven of my own—"

"Oh, I couldn't—"

"Nonsense, child. You come on over. We're good people. You need a hand. Let us help you," she urged.

Anna hesitated. She had been brought up to distrust others, to protect herself. But the woman's face was nothing but kind and helpful. Maybe she was a gift from God. One more red-faced wail from Jared sent her hand to the door handle. "Maybe just for a moment."

"Sure. Just for a moment. Get some warm food in you and that baby, and you'll feel much better."

CHAPTER TWELVE

Jared was on the last wall of the piles of newspaper clippings, magazines, and things that his great-uncle had left behind to sift through.
It was a good thing, too. The workmen were scheduled to arrive
soon to install the new windows, countertops, and bath fixtures.
Within a week the old place would be fit to sell, and Jared and Nick
would pack up their things and return to their lives in the East.

He drove any thought of Eden out of his mind. Any future with
her was impossible. They were too different. His life was too complicated. She didn't need him. But again and again he found himself
holding an item he'd already sorted because his thoughts were a half-
mile away in a tiny cottage. Eden had to be home by now. She had
to. But she had not come to him. Clearly she didn't want to pursue
anything with him either. But, he rationalized, what was the hurt in
checking up on her? Finding out how the art show went? As a
friend?

"Dad? Dad!" Nick said, running inside the cabin as if he had
something earth-shattering to tell his father.

"What?" Jared asked, wearily rubbing his eyes.

"Can I build a raft with Michael?"

"A raft? Will that be safe?"

"Sure."

"Well, I guess it's okay. But either Mr. Sundquist or I have to check it out before you go out on the water with it. Got it?"

"Got it."

"And no trial runs without a life jacket. Deal?" The river had gone down quite a bit with the summer heat eating at it, and there were few "rapids" left along its path. *Still...*

"Deal."

"What are you going to use for materials?"

"His dad said we could use the old lumber he had extra from his barn. We found some old Styrofoam blocks down by the river. Michael says they're probably from an old dock along the lake. And we're using his old surfboard from the dump in the middle. Do we have a hammer?"

"Look out in the shed. I think I saw some old tools hanging on the west wall."

Nick was gone before Jared could say another word. Taking a sip of coffee, Jared pushed thoughts of Eden away and turned back to the tiresome stack of junk. There had been few treasures worth saving in the piles but enough to make him paranoid about tossing the rest. He threw a dusty 1971 copy of *Time* to the "dump" heap and then a baggie full of never-redeemed Good Housekeeping seals saved for some prize. He paused at what came next: a brown leather purse, heavily water stained. Since Rudy had never married, Jared suspected there were few women who would have brought a purse and left it at his home. Hesitantly he reached for the pocketbook but then pulled away, fearful of what he might find. Concentrating, he reached for it again, opening the clasp even as he brought it near, afraid that he might lose his nerve. There was little inside. A cosmetic pouch full of cheap dimestore makeup too old to even be moldy. A wavy wad of Kleenex that had been doused with water and allowed to dry and harden as it lay in the bumpy contours of the purse, giving it an eerily frozen-in-time look.

Jared knew, even before he got to the wallet, that he was looking at his mother's purse. The one that had been in the car that day it plunged into the river. It had probably washed ashore downriver and been returned by some sorrowful neighbor unable to quite meet Rudy's eye.

With a shaking hand Jared pulled out a mismatched wallet and stared at his mother's blurred image on her driver's license. The water had made its way under the wallet's plastic lining as it had eventually made its way into her lungs, suffocating her, snuffing out her life.

He dropped the wallet to the floor, as horrified as if he had found himself holding her cold, wet hand. The driver's license lay on the floor, faceup. He stared at her picture, her smiling face. She had been so young. So innocent. So full of hope for the future. And then she was gone.

Jared could see the old Buick, could visualize it in his mind's eye as it filled with water, his mother pinned beneath a cruel timber. It was in the days before car seats. He had probably been riding beside her, which ultimately saved him. She still freed him, even scared and in pain, shouting for help. Her purse floating to the surface at first, maybe even floating out and downstream through a shattered window. While his mother remained, pinned, dying. Or maybe it came out when the old man had pulled Jared free of the wreckage… His tiny toes may have brushed past it, edged it out into the course of the river. Even as his mother died.

There was nothing else in the purse. A wallet, some makeup, a couple of dried out tissues. There might have been more at one point, but no longer. With a heavy heart, his eyes went to the next item on the stack, a yellowed newspaper clipping. The headline stunned him: CONWAY, POWELL DEAD IN TRAGIC BRIDGE ACCIDENT. He reread it two, then three times, then scanned the text that began, "Ernie Powell died this morning at the age of eighty-five after saving the young son of the late Anna Conway of Minneapolis, Minnesota…"

Ernie Powell. The old man. A Powell. A *Powell*.

Jared rose. He needed to go for a run. He needed to see Eden.

Angrily he tied his running shoes, wondering how she had not found the time to tell him the truth. Why had she not told him? Thinking back, he could see her expression again on the dock, that night he had the uncanny feeling that she *knew*. He went out the door, slamming it behind him. He turned, opened it, and slammed it again. And again. And again.

His anger spent, he leaned his forehead against it, panting. Nicolaus ran up with Michael trailing behind. "Dad, are you okay?"

"Fine. I'm fine," he said, not daring to turn and let his son see the tears on his cheeks. Quickly he wiped them away as if they were sweat and fiddled with the door as if repairing it. "There. I think all is in order now. What are you two up to?"

"We're looking for a few more pieces of wood for our raft."

"Remember—"

"Life jackets. I know, Dad."

"All right. I'm heading out for a run. You'll be okay for an hour?"

"Yeah."

"Keep the Sundquist's cabin in sight."

"I know, Dad. 'Bye."

"'Bye." Jared set off toward Eden's. He wasn't angry at her, couldn't be angry at her. She, too, had lost someone in that accident. Her great-grandfather, he guessed. Still, he wanted to see her. Had to see her. In minutes he had crossed the bridge and was making his way down her road, then up her driveway.

She was on the porch working when he arrived, never having made faster time. But she was not at the wheel spinning plates. She was on the floor, working on a three-quarter-scale sculpture of a woman—a woman with her hands to her sides and her face uplifted, as if looking, joyfully, at the sky, bathing in starlight. The figure was only roughed out, but already he could see that much within it. As much as the hiding woman in the shed conveyed powerful emotions of fear, this one emanated sheer joy. In spite of himself, Jared smiled.

Eden still had not looked up, so lost was she in the moment of bringing clay to life, like God breathing life into Adam. It suddenly reminded Jared of a sermon Father Frank had given in Buckley's chapel. "Imagine, if you will, the moment," he had said, pausing to show the boys his hands, cupped before him, "when God breathed life into the clay, making man." He had *huffed* into his hands and then brought them back and away, his eyes lit with wonder, and proclaimed, "Man! See him! My perfect creation!"

Eden, God-follower, was echoing his creation.

He tore his eyes from the sculpture to study the sculptor. Her brow was furrowed in concentration, her arms covered in slip to the elbows. She was sitting with a leg to either side of the sculpture, her soft cotton dress pulled up to her knees, dotted with red-brown clay, her hair constantly slipping before her eyes. He cleared his throat, and she looked up quickly, obviously startled. "Jared! I didn't hear you come up."

She rose then, looking as though she meant to cover up her work, but the sheer size of it made her impulse futile. "Well," she said, bringing one hand up nervously to brush away her hair but then catching herself, letting it dangle at her side. "What do you think?"

Jared opened the screen door and slowly climbed the three steps. "She's wonderful. Almost as wonderful as the figure in the shed."

"The shed?" Her eyes had a look of suspicion and betrayal.

"Wait a minute," he said, holding up his hands. "The door blew open while you were gone. I was just shutting it—looking after the place as you had asked me to—when I saw her. I couldn't help myself. She *drew* me."

Eden studied him, weighing things in her mind. He could see it on her face as clearly as he could watch a storm race down the lake, allowing sun to peek through in spots, drenching others with rain. Finally she ventured, "Really?"

"Really." He sank down heavily into an old rattan chair at the small coffee table and then shook his head. His questions about Ernie Powell would wait. How did a person bring up such a thing anyway? Somehow he knew this was more important. "I don't know why you don't just do this. Why the plates at all? Isn't this what inspires you, drives you?"

She sat back and considered the figure before her. "Lately, it *is* what drives me. But I have to eat," she tried.

"Sell these, and you'll eat like a queen. Let me take them back to New York with me, show them to a few people—"

"No, I don't think so. These are for me."

"Like those in your studio upstairs? When are you going to venture out, Eden? When are you going to let the world see what your God has created in you? How he has gifted you?"

She looked down at her skirt and then rose. She gave him a half-

smile. "Soon, actually. I think. I have you to thank for that, I suppose. In the midst of lecturing you the other night on the dock, I
discovered something in me that I didn't like."

"What?"

"That I have crossed one bridge, only to find myself on the
brink of another." She went to the porch railing, her hand resting against the screening, looking out upon the lake. "I was hurt on
that wedding day that never was. I let it close me off…close me
down, in a way. I don't want to be closed down, Jared." Eden turned
to him then, her eyes wet with tears, and gestured toward the figure.
"I want to be like her, open and adoring and daring to be so. Each
and every day."

Jared watched her, moved toward her. There was electricity in
the air, like the ozone during a lightning storm. He made a decision
then, acting on an impulse he had pushed away twenty-odd times
before. Crossing the span between them, he gently pulled her close,
running his hands down her cheeks, over her brow bone, through
her hair, before quietly, softly kissing her.

She was ready for him, accepting his kiss, his touch, melding to
him as if they had done so a hundred times before. He kissed her
more deeply, searching, desiring, wanting to know her in every way
possible. Without pause she returned his ardor, moving closer, holding him tightly. He pulled away after a moment more, stunned by
the magnetism between them. She raised a hand to her lip, as if
wondering about the same thing.

"I have to leave soon," he said simply.

"I know."

"End of this week, beginning of next. But soon."

"I know." There was the seed of hope in her eyes, as well as that of hurt. Hope that they might find a way between their separate lives, hurt that he was going to leave her, had to leave her.

"I'm sorry," he muttered. "I shouldn't have kissed you." He hurried off the porch and down the road, aching with each step he placed between them and yet breathing a little easier. Eden was a complication he had not anticipated in coming to Montana.

Eden allowed a couple of days to go by before she ventured down the road to Rudy's house. Hopping in her truck, she considered the tarnished urn in her hands, her excuse for stopping by. She loved the old thing and had taken to picking her own wildflowers through the summer to fill it when Jared's had faded, died, and were discarded. But at least it gave her a reason to see him, maybe even for the last time. She couldn't bear the thought that he might leave Montana, not without the chance to speak to him again.

When she drove down Rudy's old road, she admired the cleaned-up grounds. She pulled to a stop, noting workmen on the roof and others at the picture window in front, installing new glass. Getting it ready to sell. Nick was coming out of the shed and waved at her when he spotted her. She climbed out of the truck.

"Eden!" the boy called. "Come and see our raft!"

"Your raft? I'd love to. But is your dad at home?"

"He's inside! But come down and see the raft first!"

"Okay, okay," she said, grinning as the boy practically pulled her down the path to the tiny old dock on the river. Michael was down there already, busily pounding at a nail that was bent in two, the victim of an errant swing.

"Now, this is something," she said, lifting her eyebrows appreciatively. The boards were rough hewn and less than orderly in their layout on the crossboards. She could see the yellowed, disintegrating foam beneath, obviously salvaged, and laughed. "You know, we did the same thing when I was your age. Made a raft and then took it downriver."

"Cool!" Michael said, his estimation of her evidently rising. "Ours is almost ready. Then we're going to convince our dads to let us ride it down."

"It's fun. With life jackets," she added in a motherly tone. "There's only one drawback."

"What?" Nicolaus asked.

"There's no way to get a raft this size back upriver, unless you pole it back up, which—believe me—is very hard work."

"What'd you do with yours?" Michael asked.

"We decided one good run was worth it and took it down to where the highway meets the river again, right across from that clear-cut. We left it there, hoping some other kids would find it and play with it."

"What happened to it?" Nick asked.

"I don't know. It stayed there for a while. Either some kids found it, or it drifted all the way down to the dam during the spring thaw."

"Cool!"

"Did you watch it go over the waterfall?"

"No, no. They have those big nets that catch all the debris before the dam. Maybe it made it all the way to the nets. Maybe the guy who cleared the nets brought it to the edge of the river to fish from."

"Yeah!"

"Or maybe some kids made it an island, keeping it in place with boulders."

"Yeah!"

She left them, then, to talk about the possibilities. Eden was still thinking about their raft and that summer when she was ten years old when she spotted Jared at the top of the hill. Their eyes met for an awkward, intimate moment.

"Think it's seaworthy?"

"It's questionable," she said with a laugh. "I didn't dare to step aboard." He turned, and she followed him. "Are you going to let them ride it?"

"I don't know. I'll have to talk to the Sundquists. Maybe if one of us rode along."

"The river's pretty low now," she encouraged. "They'd probably have to portage it in places."

"Better that than run the rapids on old foam and lumber."

She laughed again. "I'd agree with that." They reached the outside of the cabin. "Looks like the workmen are wrapping up the work on the old place."

"Yeah, some basic stuff. Windows, counters, new bath fixtures. I'm almost ready to put it on the market."

She looked at him then, noting the sorrow in his voice. "Why don't you keep it?" She turned away, trying to appear more interested in the moss clinging to the roof's shingles than his response.

"Thought of that," he said, kicking his toe into the loamy ground of the forest floor. "Decided it was too far. I'm afraid I wouldn't get here enough to make it worth it."

She swallowed hard at his words.

She wasn't worth it; *she* was too far.

"Yes, well, I just stopped by to give you this." She walked to the truck, swallowing hard again against the burning in her throat. She didn't want to cry, not now. He followed her. Eden reached through the window and grabbed the urn and pulled it out, offering it to him.

"No, Eden," he protested. "That's for you."

"Oh, the flowers were enough. Come on, it's probably worth something." She lifted it again.

But he refused. "No, no. You keep it. I want you to have it."

She gave him a half-nod and pulled it close. "Well, I can't send you off empty-handed. Why don't you and Nick come over tomorrow and each make a pot? We'll fire them, and you can take them home with you. A little piece of Montana clay you can keep forever."

A little piece of me.

When he hesitated, she asked, "You're not going right away, right? You still have a few days?" She hated the urgency in her voice. "Because it'll take a couple days to fire and glaze it," she amended.

He ran a hand through his hair and stared at her. "I don't know, Eden."

"Oh, hey, it's just a pot. It's no big deal if you'd rather not. You probably have a lot to do before—"

"I'll be there tomorrow. Ten o'clock, okay?" He looked torn, anguished.

"Sure," she said, staring into his eyes. "Ten o'clock."

Anna's heart sang as they crossed the eastern Montana border. The vistas were broad—miles long. There wasn't much to stop one's vision in this part of the state. But she was heading to Uncle Rudy's, to a snug little cabin of safety. Uncle Rudy had always been there for her with a kind word, a thoughtful insight. When she had written to him, asking if she and Jared could stay with him for a while, he had welcomed her without questions.

Not like her parents might have done, had they been alive. Mama and Papa had always been so judgmental, so harsh. They would have never understood her love for Rick, her fall into disgrace. They had always been so…perfect. No doubt they would have disowned her.

But not Uncle Rudy. His words from the letter encouraged her onward, beckoned her toward the river: "Come, child. Bring the babe. All will be well. We will see to it." She chanted it as a mantra. The words helped distract her as the miles of pavement disappeared beneath her threadbare tires and Jared cried for hours at a time. Despite her every attempt to appease the baby, to distract him with various trinkets, her child was clearly tired of riding in the car. After three days she was too.

If it hadn't been for the kindly woman and man who offered her dinner in South Dakota, she wouldn't have made it this far at all. They had not only fed her the night before but also bought milk for the baby and slipped her a twenty—a "loan" they called it—including their address with the neatly folded bill. This morning her milk had returned, enough to keep Jared satisfied. And Uncle Rudy… If it hadn't been for him, she wouldn't have had anywhere to go. God was looking out for her. For the first time in a very long time, she was sure of it.

Here she was on the border of Montana! Even with so many miles left, just being in the state of her destination did her heart some serious good.

CHAPTER THIRTEEN

"I'm coming, Jared," she said over the phone. "I'll be there Tuesday. Have him ready."

Jared sighed. "Patricia, that's not necessary. We'll be home in a week."

"That's what you've been saying all summer! It's been more than two months since you picked him up from school, and I haven't seen him in over a month."

"Look, I'm sorry. This time has been so good for us. I just couldn't get myself to leave. I kept thinking, 'Next week, we'll head home.' Honestly. I wasn't lying."

"Well, now his summer vacation is over, and I've barely seen him."

"Oh, come on! Don't tell me you've been sitting around twiddling your thumbs. You weren't thinking about our son while you were in Tahiti." Nick had tried to get ahold of his mother for a week. Finally a maid had answered the phone and told him where she was.

"That's not fair."

Jared sighed again. "No. You're right. But please don't play the woebegone mother with me when at the start of the summer you barely cared if you saw him at all." He spotted Nick then, peeking around the corner, and winced. "Oh, *man*…Nick!" The boy was running out the door. "Patricia, I have to go. I'll call you back."

"Jared! He heard you? I'll see you on Tuesday. Have him ready—"

"Patricia! I'm telling you, we're coming home." A workman came through, carrying the new bathroom sink, and Jared lowered his voice. "I'm doing a few improvements, and it'll be on the market in—"

"Tuesday, Jared. I'm flying him home. Have him ready, or I'm calling the attorney."

"Don't come, Patricia. We won't be here. We'll be on the road."

"I don't believe you."

"Believe me. We'll be leaving mid—"

The line went dead.

Jared hung up the phone heavily. He had wanted the time with Nick on the way back to New York, wanted those last days on the road with him before he went back to Buckley. And the last thing he wanted was Patricia here, on the river. He wanted nothing but the summer's memories of this place filling his head, not the arguments that were sure to come along with his ex-wife. But he couldn't worry about it now. Now he had to go and find Nicolaus and make sure his words had not done irreparable damage.

"So then I asked him if he and Nick wanted to come over and make a pot—my lame attempt to see him again, I guess," Eden said to Renee, who was leaning across her counter at the gallery.

"Did he say yes?"

"Kind of. You could see it in his eyes; his heart was saying yes, and his head was saying no."

"I think it's a good sign that he went with his heart."

"Yeah, well, so what?" Eden said, throwing her hand in the air, then pacing about the gallery, picking up pieces she was not really looking at. "So, let's say he comes over tomorrow morning and we make his pot. Then I fire it, and then he comes back over to glaze it, and then I fire it again, and then I have an excuse to go over to see him one last time. I'm an idiot. It will just prolong the inevitable and make me more crazy."

"*More* crazy?"

"Yes, even *more*," she said, ignoring Renee's jibe. She sat down heavily. "I knew I shouldn't have gotten involved with him. I knew I shouldn't let my guard down."

"No," Renee said, coming around and placing a gentle hand on her shoulder. "You knew it was time to try."

Eden nodded. "I want you to do something, Renee."

"What?"

"I'm going to glaze my 'troubled woman' figure this weekend, then another you haven't seen yet. Will you put them out? Do you have room?"

Renee stared at her. "I think I've been making room for them all summer, girl. What changed your mind?"

"I'm not quite sure. I guess when I woke up that time with the figure in my head—when I knew she couldn't be anything but three-quarter scale—I knew I was going to have to venture further than ever before."

"Think it's God pushing you out of your comfort zone?"

"Let's hope so. I'd hate to think of the alternative."

"And what of Jared's offer to take them to New York? To show them to some friends there?"

Eden studied her, Renee's expression revealing how it hurt her to sacrifice showing the figures at her little gallery in order to help Eden's career. But this wasn't about her career; it was about venturing out into life. "No. They belong here, Renee. With you."

Relief washed over the woman's face. "Oh, good! When can I get them? In a few days?"

Eden nodded. "From what I can gather, Jared and his son will be gone by then. That seems right to me. I'll say good-bye to Jared and then move on. I'll cross my own bridge."

Renee nodded too, sorrow in her eyes. "Listen, maybe he'll be back."

"I don't think so. He's selling Rudy's place. He told me that Montana is too far from New York to visit."

"But he kissed you."

"And said he should never have done so." She plastered a smile on her face. "It'll be okay, Renee. I'll be okay."

Her friend reached across the counter and squeezed her hand. "Yes you will, Eden. Somehow, you will."

"Where's Nick?" Eden asked, wiping her hands on a towel thrown over her shoulder as Jared came inside the kitchen door.

"I'm sorry. He's not coming," Jared said, suddenly feeling uncomfortable, vulnerable alone with her again. "Michael asked him along to town with his family, and Nicolaus wanted to go, so I said yes. It's about killing him to say good-bye to the boy."

As it's killing me to let us go, he thought.

Eden looked at him quickly, as if she could hear him. She turned away. "Want some breakfast? I just made some fresh granola."

"Sounds good," he allowed. He sat down at her counter.

"Coffee?"

"Please." He watched as she poured the cup, wanting to memorize every inch of her fingers, her wrists, her forearms—all of her. "Do you have an extra picture around, Eden…of you?"

She laughed. "Not any that aren't ten years old."

"Oh. That's too bad. I would've liked to take one with me."

She smiled sadly. "I've always found that memories are kinder than photos."

"But memories fade."

Eden nodded slightly, her expression growing a little more sorrowful, then met his eyes. "I'll always remember this summer as a good one, Jared."

"As will I, Eden."

They chatted over their breakfast of granola—about how the work on Rudy's cabin, scheduled to be completed that day, was going; about Nick's trip down the river, which went without incident; about how the fish weren't biting much lately. Anything to avoid discussing his departure any further.

"Come on," she said, rising. "Let's go make a pot for you to take home to New York. Something for you to remember your summer on the Swan by."

"As if I could ever forget it."

Eden gathered sponges, water, leather, wire and other necessities from the attic studio before joining Jared on the porch. He was admiring her "joy woman" when she came out. He immediately rushed forward to help ease her overburdened arms. "Here, let me help."

They set all the materials on the picnic bench, which was spread with a plastic cloth. She unwrapped the clay and, using the wire, cut off a section for Jared. "Here. Form it into a wedged ball, like a loose haystack."

He set to work as instructed. "Can I use this?" he asked, picking up a knife.

"Certainly." She moved away to moisten the plaster bat of the wheel and grab her apron from behind the door.

"Like this?" he asked, holding it up.

"Perfect." She motioned toward the wheel as she knotted the apron ties behind her. "Want an apron before we begin throwing the pot?"

"We're going to be throwing pots?" he asked with a teasing smile.

"You know the lingo," she said lightly.

"A little. Did it once in college art class."

"Okay, college boy. No apron?"

"No need. Wore my grubbies."

She sat down across from him as he sat down in the seat of the kick wheel, his knees touching hers. "Now slap that hunk of clay dead center on the wheel."

"Like that?"

"Yes. Now you kick the wheel like this to get it going. That's it. After you get the clay into a beehive shape, it doesn't take much to keep it going. Here, wet your hands." She lifted a ceramic bowl she had made, full of warm water.

"Trying to intimidate me with that?" he asked, another smile lighting up his eyes.

"Hardly," she laughed under her breath. "I did that in high school."

"Okay," he said, staring at the smooth ball under his hands as he awkwardly pushed at the wheel with his foot. "Now I am *really* intimidated."

She smiled. "Brace your elbows against your knees," she said, studying his long fingers, covered in slip as they seemed to caress the contours of the clay beneath his hands. "Good. You'll need that steady leverage. Now gently dig in your thumbs. Softer! That's it, gently. Yes, keep the pressure even with both thumbs. There you go."

He laughed. "I'd forgotten how fun this is!" The clay's depression, in the center, grew, while the rounded walls became thicker.

"Here. Wet your hands again."

He did so obediently, then set back to work on the pot. When the depression reached the bottom, he looked up at her expectantly. "Now what?"

"Let me show you." Using her thumb and fingers, she opened up the center, thinning and raising the walls with her knuckle on the outside as she urged them upward.

"I see. Let me try."

He slowed the wheel, running his hands over and over the same clay, overworking it, and the pot's wall soon slumped.

"No worries," she said, smiling her encouragement. "Here, we'll just rebuild it and see if we can't salvage it." She could feel his eyes on her as much as their creation, but she refused to look up. Rising, she cleared the water that had collected at the bottom of the pot, making the clay too soft, and then sat down again. "There. Now let's try it again. Wet your hands."

She set her fingers on his, still resolutely staring at the pot. "This is the pressure I want you to use," she said, guiding his hands with her own. Jared kicked the wheel faster and faster, seemingly mesmerized with their project. Red-brown slip soon covered their fingers as they worked. "There you go. A bit harder now." Beneath their hands the walls of the pot rose, rounding in the middle, and after Eden shaved some off with a wooden rib, they "necked in," or narrowed the top.

The wheel slowed. The pot was nearly perfect. A tiny bit lopsided, but nearly perfect. "I like it," she said, leaning back in her chair.

"I do too," he said with a grin, nodding his pleasure.

Eden leaned forward and looked first at one side, then the other. "I'll let it dry a bit now, before trimming it from the bat."

"So, we're done?"

There was no reason to keep him. "For now. We let it dry until it's about as hard as leather, and then do some trimming."

"I suppose you would be better at that than I. You hardly need me here for that step. What's after that?"

"Well...I...I'll bisque fire it, then you could come back and glaze. I'll fire it again, it'll cool, and you'll have yourself a pot. I was thinking I'd fire it tomorrow. You could come over the next day to glaze if you'd like."

"What day is that? Sunday?" He was withdrawing from her. She could feel it. "Sunday's not good. Nick and I are going up to that church near Lake MacDonald and then taking a hike. Last hurrah and all."

"I see. What about Monday?"

He squinted his eyes and then looked at her regretfully. "Sorry. I think we'll be packing that day."

"So...you're leaving Tuesday?"

"Or Wednesday. Sometime soon." He met her gaze for a moment and then rose. "I had better get going. Thanks for the lesson. I'll trust the expert to finish the pot."

"You're welcome." She rose too. Half of her wanted to go to him, to kiss him, to remind him of the promise of what they had discovered together, and the other half felt like running away. From her own home, from the place she had always felt safest. She swallowed hard, trying to ask her next question in a tone that added no pressure. "Will I see you before you go?"

He had washed his hands in the bowl and wiped them on a towel at the table. She followed him out the screen door and down the stairs, trying to hold back, not appear overeager.

"I don't know, Eden." He ran his hand through his hair and looked out at the lake, then back to her. "Part of me wants to. The other part just thinks it prolongs the pain." Gently he took her hand and looked into her eyes. "I'm no good for you, Eden."

"Why do you say that?"

"I have too much to get straight. Your life here is so good, so right. I'd just mess it all up."

My life is too straight, too narrow, she thought. *Mess it up. Please mess it up.*

He dropped her hand then. "I'll see you before I go," he promised, walking away backward, still facing her.

Then he turned on his heel, reached his BMW, and left, driving too fancy a car for a gravel road.

On Sunday, Eden took Gram out to church and then to brunch, trying to keep her mind off of Jared and Nick leaving. It was pouring rain, as it had been for days, soaking the ground, encasing the valley in a shroud of gray.

"So he's going? What's wrong with the man?" Gram asked, sitting beside her in the truck as they drove to the café.

"Not every man falls head over heels in love when they meet me," Eden quipped.

"A man with any sense would," the old woman said, incensed.

"Jared...Jared's got some things to work out in his head yet."

"So you're hoping he'll come back?"

"I don't think so. Rudy's place is up for sale. Jared has an entire life in New York—his work, his son, his...life."

"Seems to me a man could move his work and his son to Montana."

"Not necessarily, Gram. That's a big step, and Bigfork isn't exactly a hotbed for commodities brokers."

"Can't they live anywhere these days? Telecommute?"

Eden glanced at her with a wry smile.

"What? An old woman can read *Time* as well as a young woman."

"Yes, I suppose he could telecommute. But maybe he doesn't want to. The river is...quiet. It has to be the opposite of everything he knows in New York."

"*Hmph.* I still think the man is thickheaded if he's started something with you and is ready to just walk off and leave. He obviously doesn't know what he has," her tone making Eden feel like a queen for a moment.

She sighed. "I don't know, Gram. Maybe I got it wrong. Maybe we never really started anything at all."

"What's the matter, Dad?" Nick asked as he cast his fly into the still waters of Lake MacDonald.

"Nothing. Why do you ask?" Jared cast alongside his son. The fish weren't biting, but the two were content just to be together on the remote stretch of beach, Glacier's peaks towering above them, reflecting snowcapped tops in the cobalt blue lake.

"You're pretty quiet."

"Just thinking. It seems like I have a lot of thinking to do these days."

The boy nodded sagely, as if he had his own share of thinking to do.

"Nick," his father asked suddenly, "how badly do you want to return to Buckley?"

The boy paused midcast, his line pooling before him. "Why? What do you mean?"

"What...what if you came home with me instead? Went to school in the city?"

"I don't know. All my friends are at Buckley. They're probably all wondering where I am, with term starting next week and all."

"Yeah. We should get home this week so you're ready. I understand that your friends are all there."

"Dad?"

"Yeah?"

"What if...what if we stayed here?"

Jared raised his eyebrows. What was once a question he would have dismissed immediately as ludicrous was now one he had asked himself a hundred times. "We can't, Son. My work, your mom, your school—it's all in New York."

"Yeah." His voice was disappointed. "I like it here. I like being with you."

"So do I, Nick. It's been a good summer, huh?"

"The best."

"Maybe we can come back next summer. Not for so long, but for a vacation at least."

"Maybe." The boy sounded as if it would never compare. Jared knew it would not. "We won't be able to stay at the cabin."

"No," Jared agreed. "It will have sold by then, I'm pretty sure."

"I like living next to Michael."

"I know. Maybe the next place we stay in will have another neighbor kid."

"But it won't be Michael."

"No." Jared swallowed hard around a lump in his throat. What was wrong with him? Getting as upset as his boy over leaving the neighbors? He shook his head and pulled in his line. "C'mon, let's take a drive up the pass. Eden said...Eden said we shouldn't miss it."

"Okay." Nicolaus brought in his line and glanced at his father. "Dad?"

"Yeah?"

"You going to miss Eden?"

Jared looked down at the fine, rounded silver and gray-blue gravel at his feet and then back to his son. "Yes, I suppose I am."

"Even more than I'm going to miss Michael?"

Jared nodded slightly. "Probably even more."

Nick took Jared's hand as they walked back toward the car, surprising him. "It's hard moving away, isn't it?"

Eden held out until Tuesday. By that afternoon she could barely handle the suspense. Had Jared left already? Without saying good-bye? After all, he had said it would be Tuesday or Wednesday...and that he would come to say good-bye. Repeatedly she told herself she couldn't go to see him, shouldn't go to see him. That he would come to see her if he was worth his salt. But when Eden went to her kiln and pulled out the slightly lopsided, bisque-glazed pot and a skiff of other pottery, it was the pot that she went to over and over again.

She carried it with her to the beach, lifting her face to the wind off the lake, wondering at the cooling hint of autumn on the wet breeze even though it was still August. She remembered his hands on the pot's slippery surface—and that last day together. She remembered how he had held her hand and told her he was no good for her. He clearly could not move forward with her, didn't want to move forward. She just had to accept it. It wasn't meant to be.

Eden looked back to the pot, feeling the crisp, prickly surface of the bisque. Maybe he had changed his mind. About the pot. Maybe he wanted to glaze it himself. Or maybe he didn't even want it at all.

She climbed the hill to the cabin, went to the phone in the kitchen, lifted the heavy receiver off of the hook, then paused, and finally replaced it. If she called, he might just say no. If she dropped by, he might say yes. And she wanted him to say yes. Yes to one last hour together, if nothing else.

Long, shapely calves in stockings and heels was all he saw, but he would've known his ex-wife's legs anywhere. He sighed and let the new curtains fall back over his bedroom window as he heard Nick shout in excitement. "Dad! Dad! It's Mom! She's here!" Nick ran through the cabin and slammed the front door behind him as he dashed out into the rain. Any trepidation that Jared felt about her arrival was obviously not shared by his son, and he felt a twinge of guilt for keeping the boy from her.

She had arrived by cab, probably paying a small fortune—even by New York standards—for the fare from the Kalispell airport to their cabin, forty minutes distant. Jared paused and took a deep breath. Patricia's arrival certainly meant conflict on the horizon. If she had only waited. They were so close to leaving—the drive home would've been the perfect end to a perfect summer. And now Patricia was going to ruin it all.

He willed himself to the front door and out, forcing a smile to his face. "You came," he said lightly as she took her small suitcase from the driver, paid the man, and then turned to Jared.

"As I said I would."

"I thought I said we were heading home tomorrow."

She covered her hair with a leather briefcase and dashed toward them. "I came to make sure," she said, giving Nicolaus another hug. "Perhaps we can all ride together."

"You hate road trips!" Jared said with a laugh.

"Yes, I do. I just want to see you on the road and heading east. You can drop Nick and me at the airport."

"I said I was bringing him home in a couple of days…" Jared tried to keep his tone pleasant.

"As you've been saying all summer long."

"Mom! Mom! I've learned how to fly-fish!"

"Have you now? Who taught you?"

"Dad! And Eden! Want to see? Come on! I'll show you down by the river!"

"I'd better change first, darling. Let me get into something else, and we'll come down for the show. You had better get it all in tonight, though, sweetheart." She knelt before Nick and stroked his sweet, innocent face. "My goodness, look at you! You're as brown as a berry! Has your father put any sunscreen on you this summer at all?"

"A little."

"Oh, well. I suppose you were outdoors from sunup to sundown?"

"Mostly."

"Did your dad tell you we're leaving tomorrow?"

Nick threw his father a confused look. "He said *we're* leaving."

"Oh, good." She rose. "If you'll show me to your bathroom, Jared, I'll change and get Nick out of your hair. So you can *pack*," she said as she passed him.

Sighing, Jared followed her and patted Nick reassuringly on the back.

"How…quaint. Very rustic. I do hope it hasn't affected Nicolaus's allergies."

"He's been fine. All summer."

"Oh. Well, good. It'd probably take forever to get him to a hospital if he had one of his asthma attacks."

"The only time he had an asthma attack was when you dragged him through the perfume bar at Macy's."

"You never know when another will strike. Particularly in a rain forest like this," she said, peering out the window at the mist.

Jared stared at her for a moment. "The bathroom's over there."

"I'll be down at the dock, Mom! Setting up!" Nick said, ignoring the obvious tension between his parents.

"Don't you want to wait until…? Oh, all right. I'll be right down," she looked up at Jared, meeting his challenge, just as she always had.

Some things never change, he thought.

He turned away first, wanting her out of the cabin. While she was down at the dock, he would call the lodge in Bigfork to see if there was a room available for her for the night. He heard the bathroom door click as he went to the big picture window. His mind and his pulse rate were spinning; Patricia always did that to him. Made him crazy. He concentrated on the river, visualizing himself in Eden's prayer spot among the birch, beneath the aspens and cottonwoods. He could almost smell the sun-hot rocks and see a crane swoop low over the water with its giant wingspan and crooked, awkward neck.

A knock at the front door brought him back to the present. Frowning, he turned toward it. All the work in the kitchen and bath was complete; he didn't expect anyone until tomorrow morning, when Julie Vose was dropping by to get the house key as he departed. Crossing the hardwood floor, he opened the old door.

It was Eden. She looked up at him sheepishly, a bone-white pot in her hands. "I should've called," she said, awkwardly motioning over her shoulder at the truck in the drive, staring into his eyes. "But then I thought I'd just swing by… This isn't a good time, is it?" She lowered her brow and shook her head a little, obviously reading the tension on his face.

He smiled and shook his head with a slight grimace. "I was going to come by anyway—"

"Oh, good. I was wondering if you really wanted to glaze this or if—"

"Jared?" Patricia called. "Do you have a spare washcloth and towel?"

Eden frowned, confused at the sound of a woman's voice. "I…I'm sorry. I should've called." She turned to go. "I'll catch you later."

"No, Eden. Wait."

"Jared?" Patricia called. "Are they here, in the closet?"

Eden glanced back, her face filled with betrayal.

"Honestly," Patricia said, approaching the front door. "Oh, someone's here." She glanced out the window and spotted Eden.

Eden rushed to her truck and quickly opened the door. It was then that the pot slipped from her hands, cracking on a large rock in the driveway.

"Oh!" she cried.

She knelt and Jared came out to her. "Shoot," Jared commiserated, as miserable as she that the pot they had created together was ruined.

"I'm sorry…I was stupid to have brought it over. I was stupid to come here."

"No, no you weren't." They rose together. "Eden, she's my ex-wife."

Eden nodded, her eyes still clouded by confusion. The mist was coating her hair, dragging it over her eyes.

"She's here because of Nick. Let me explain. I'll come over later. Okay?"

She stared at him for a moment and then shook her head slightly. "You don't need to explain, Jared." She paused a moment. "Let's just say good-bye now. Take care of yourself."

"You can say good-bye now, but I'm coming over later, even if I have to talk to your empty front porch."

"Suit yourself," she said, feigning indifference. But she cared. If she didn't, she wouldn't have fabricated the excuse to come over. He slammed the truck door behind her.

"I'll be over. Later. After Nick's in bed. All right?"

"Sure. If that's the best thing." *So cool,* he thought. *Protecting herself. As she should. I'm going to hurt her. I've already hurt her.*

"I'll see you tonight, Eden Powell." He stood there in the drive until she disappeared down the road, covered by the protecting walls of the forest as she had been most of her life. Then he turned back to deal with his ex-wife.

Anna leaned against the wide steering wheel and wept as steam poured from under the hood. It was a hot day, and the car had overheated. The baby was just as uncomfortable, sitting up and screaming when she tried to keep him in the bassinet beside her. She looked at him, her vision blurred by her tears. Little tendrils of hair curled in wet ringlets about his red face. He always got flushed when he squalled in anger. Alternately sighing, then gasping for air, she lifted him out from the basket, pulled him toward her, and then opened the heavy, wide Buick door.

She stood outside, still crying, her fury growing. "Why?" she screamed at the sky. "I'm trying to do the right thing here! The right thing. Why don't you give me a break?" The tears came faster then, and Anna sank to the ground, clutching her son to her chest. Her weeping had unnerved him, and his squalling escalated. They rocked there, on the side of the dusty, lonely road, crying together for half an hour under the blazing sun that scorched the deserted plains of eastern Montana.

"All I want is to get there," she whispered to the pale blue sky when her tears abated. She could envision the cool waters of the Swan, imagined playing with Jared there, dipping his tiny toes. Collecting rocks. She could see the stones of earth colors—clay and amber, blue the shade of sky at the end of day, turquoise green. All covered by the healing, welcome waters of the Swan. She had grown up visiting Uncle Rudy and his cabin with her father, spending several weeks every summer along its banks. There was a sense of peace there, home. It was the only place Anna felt that way. Minnesota had never been like that for her, nor had

her time in Chicago with Rick ever made any inroads in her heart. It was Montana that captivated her, held her, called to her.

The steam from under the hood subsided, and with it, Jared's tears as well. She sighed, taking that awkward breath at the end of any good cry as the babe tucked his head in the crook of her neck, trying to get his own breath. "Well, my boy, here we are. About fifty miles from the nearest Podunk town with one more hurdle in our path. Someone doesn't want us to get to Uncle Rudy's."

CHAPTER FOURTEEN

It was eleven o'clock before Jared could extricate himself from Nick and Patricia. After looking in on his son, who was huddled beneath heavy blankets, Jared padded out to the living room and grabbed his jacket. "I tried to get you a room in town, but everything was booked. You can sleep on our couch tonight."

"How chivalrous. Where are you going?" Patricia asked, paging through a copy of *In Style*. She was sitting by the fire to ward off the evening chill, her legs pulled up in the big, overstuffed plaid chair. She looked like a model from the magazine she read.

"Out," he said, resolutely turning away.

"To see her. In this weather," she commented, still staring at her magazine as if uninterested.

"Yes," he said simply. He left, shutting the door firmly behind him. Looking up at the towering pines about him, he inhaled the scent of them as they waved in the night breeze. He already missed the place. The ponderosas, tamaracks, and white pines moved in a silent, ungainly dance as gust after gust moved through them. A great horned owl hooted from one of the nearby trees, and another answered. Jared strained his eyes to try to spot them among the swaying, giant trees silhouetted against a starry night sky, but failing, he moved to his car and then down the road to Eden's.

He was crossing the bridge when he spotted the figure staring down into the water. It was Eden. There was little traffic on the road at this hour, so he pulled over, shifted the gear into park, and stepped out of the car.

"Eden?"

"Yes."

"What are you doing?"

"Thinking."

Jared shut the door and walked over to where she stood, huddled in a barn coat and leaning over the railing. The rain had abated, but the river was running high again. The forest smelled damp and clean, the dust of high summer already long gone.

"It was here that I first saw you," she said.

He nodded, even though he knew she couldn't see him do so. "I spent a lot of time here this past summer." He leaned down beside her, resting his forearms on the guardrail next to her and staring at the moonlight dancing among the rivulets of gushing water, like shining, silken strands woven into one cord beneath them. "I had a lot to figure out. A lot to face."

"So, that done, you'll go now." It was more of a statement than a question.

He left it hanging, not knowing what to say that wouldn't hurt her more. He studied her in the soft light, studied her imperfect profile. It was then that he understood that he loved her, really loved her. She was beautiful, from the inside out. So different from Patricia. And those differences were good. But it was the wrong place, the wrong time for them.

"Did you know it was your great-grandfather who saved me from the river, Eden?" he asked softly.

She faltered slightly, her eyes slipping from the horizon to the glimmering water. "Yes."

"How long have you known?"

"A while."

"Why didn't you tell me?"

"I...couldn't. It was never the right time."

"He died too. That day my mother died."

"Yes."

"I'm sorry. It was your great-grandfather, right?" He stood upright, as if preparing to receive a blow.

"Yes." She rose and turned toward him.

"I'm sorry," he said again sincerely.

"It was a long time ago, Jared," she said softly, her voice just barely audible over the water beneath them. She reached up to touch his face gently. "The wounds in our family healed long ago. How about in yours?" She dropped her hand but not her gaze, not releasing him, excusing him, or giving him any line.

He didn't respond but just stared back at her, considering her question.

She nodded finally, as if that were response enough. "Why is Patricia here?"

Jared shook his head as if he could clear it of her bigger question. "To collect Nick. I think she was afraid I would stay here with him. Forever."

"Would that be so bad?" He could tell she was holding her breath.

"In many ways, no, Eden. But I have to go home. Don's been calling a lot, and there's a lot I have to take care of with the business." He shrugged his shoulders. "I'm unsettled...restless again. Patricia irritated me in her arrival, but it's all right. She's only pushing me to do what I might have put off a few more days. Making this"—he paused to motion between them—"harder."

She hesitated as though she wanted to say something but ended up saying nothing at all.

Was he hurting her? How could he do this without hurting her? He had been an idiot, starting anything…

Then without another word, Eden hugged him briefly, turned on her heel, and left him standing alone on the bridge. He watched her as she faded into the dark forest one last time, and then he shivered. Never before had the bridge felt so cold and lonely. He wanted to run after her, to say he was going to stay forever, to say he wanted to know her better and better each day. "I want to love you, Eden," he whispered. "But I can't." He felt strangled by the confusion in his heart.

With tears slipping down his cheeks, his nose running, he turned and started to walk off the bridge one last time, but the light upon the water caught his attention. He wiped his nose and sat down on a guardrail post to stare at the black, shimmering water and consider his sorrow over Eden, over his mother, over Eden's great-grandfather, Ernie Powell. What had it been like for his mother in those last few moments? For Ernie? What had they been thinking about? The longer he stared at the inky black water, the more it came to him.

Anna grinned as she turned left off of Highway 83 and onto a gravel road. "We're here, baby boy! This is where it all gets better. Where we make a new start!" She nudged her pudgy one-year-old under the chin. "You've always struck me as a Montana sort of boy anyway."

She blinked hard and yawned, weary after driving all night, and tried to focus on the road in the dim dawn light. Wouldn't Uncle Rudy be surprised that they were already here? She had thought about calling ahead but resisted, wanting to see the look on his face when she and Jared showed up on his doorstep. He had always been so kind. And he was so wonderful to welcome them as he had. It would be good here. She could feel it. "Thank you, Lord," she whispered.

Anna rolled down the window, wanting the refreshing morning air to enter in, to invigorate her. The scents of home and good memories wafted through—of dusty gravel roads, pinesap heating up with the morning, and drying prairie grass. The road curved and climbed a hill, and she glimpsed a shining bend in the river. She squealed. "Here we are, Jared! We're almost home! You've been such a good boy. Such a sweet boy," she cooed.

Jared's face dimpled in a smile at the happy sound of his mother's voice, and then he was distracted by the filtered morning light coming through the trees outside his window. "Oh, you like the trees, huh?" Anna asked, her voice still high and singsong. "There will be so many trees for you to look at here, baby. And sticks to chew on and water to play in…"

She turned one last curve, and the old bridge came into view. She slowed a bit and entered with a slight thump, spotting old Mr. Powell casting a fly. It had been years, but the man looked the same as he always had. She knew he wouldn't recognize her now, especially with a baby.

Anna smiled as the chu-chunk, chu-chunk of the first bridge cross-pieces welcomed her tires in a sound she hadn't heard in over a decade. But then there was a groaning, splitting sound that made her smile fade.

She slowed and her heart leaped as a huge crack rent the air. Was it a tree falling? The rumbling…the noise… To her horror, she felt her car being pulled backward. She screamed. By reflex she reached for Jared's bassinet but could do nothing more than hold on tight as they fell. When the car hit the water, her head slammed painfully backward, then forward, ricocheting from the impact. She screamed again for help, reaching for her baby.

Jared was so close—nearly within reach. Cold water seeped through the seat to her back, and she realized there was water in the car, that they were sinking. She shrieked in panic, desperately trying to reach Jared's bassinet, perched almost sideways against the door. The baby was wailing. They had to get out! Now!

It was then that she heard another splitting crack and looked up to see a crosspiece from the bridge fall toward the old Buick. She saw it coming, as if in slow motion, and breathed a quick prayer for her child before it slammed through the windshield, showering them with glass she didn't feel. She was hopeful that it was going to miss her, that it would come down between her and the baby. But dimly, she looked down to see that it crossed her body, pinning her against the seat in the rapidly sinking car. She felt no pain; vaguely, she wondered if she was in shock.

In a daze, she turned to Jared's bassinet, upright again, partially floating just beyond the wood that had impaled the car. He was wailing, reaching for her. "Shh, shh, baby," she whispered as if they were in a quiet nursery. The water reached her waist as she strained to grab the edge and turn it toward her. It was cold, so cold.

It was then that she felt the pain that took her breath away. She looked downward, at the dancing cloud of bright red blood pouring from a gaping wound in her abdomen. The water reached her chest as she pulled Jared to her one last time. "I...I can't believe it, baby. So close," she gasped, feeling his warm, soft skin against her neck, the tickly fuzz of his hair on her chin. "We were so close. So close!" she cried, her voice shaking as tears ran down her face. "Oh, Lord, save me! Save my baby."

Jared gasped as if he were seeing it for himself, the newspaper account coming to life before his very eyes. What had she wanted from that last moment with her child? What would it be like to give up Nick, to think that they were both on the verge of death? He gave in to the burning lump in his throat and wept.

He turned and jumped off of the guardrail post and walked down the slope to the water, wading in without pause, crying for the mother he never knew. For Eden's great-grandfather. The water reached his calves, then his thighs, then his waist. He struggled forward against the current, wanting to feel what it was they had felt. Wanting to know, to experience some of their pain. He remembered Nick's sweet face when he was a toddler, how he loved to hold the child close and rock him to sleep. He imagined himself in his mother's arms. "Oh, Mom," he cried, fresh tears rolling down his face. It was cold, so cold. And she had been in such pain...

"Oh, God!" Anna cried, sobbing with fear and pain and sorrow over what was to come. "Please, Lord! Save us! Save my child." She was holding Jared up as far as she could from the icy fingers of water that threatened them, holding her chin up as high as possible, gasping for air.

We're going to die here, she thought. Right here, in the river that I thought would bring us a new life.

The rising water covered Anna's face, and she concentrated on keeping Jared alive a moment longer instead of wasting any energy on herself. She pushed him an inch higher.

It was then that old Mr. Powell peered over the edge of the car. Even through the water, she could see his outline and a light behind him that was so bright… She released the last of the air in her lungs, pushing Jared upward, forward, to salvation. *Take him, please,* she thought. *Take him! Save him!*

Strong hands took the child from her, and impossibly light, impossibly empty now, her hands sank below the surface, still partly buoyant as they waved like the reeds of the river. She suddenly felt warm, peaceful, as if a comforting blanket fell over her. She was so weary! So tired!

"All will be well, Anna," said her Lord to her heart. *"Rest. Rest now, Anna."* And she knew it as truth.

She gave in to the water that called to her, that wanted her, that flooded her mouth and filled her lungs and then finally took her home.

Jared clung to the cement piling, visualizing a scene he had lived but could not recall, imagining the pain and anguish of those last choices of his mother and the old man. "No, Mom. Why'd you let go?" he moaned.

"No!" he shouted, as if he could force back time and what had transpired. "No," he wept through great, heaving sobs. "I wanted to *know* you. I wanted to discover life with you at my side. It wasn't fair! It wasn't fair. Why, God? Why couldn't you have saved her, too? *Why?!*"

The water rushed over him, past his shoulders as he clung to the piling and beyond, as if in silent answer. On and on it went, never stopping, seldom slowing, ever new. It was like all of life. His mother and Ernie had once been of the river, in the river, one with the river. Then they were swept away, leaving him alone to deal with their memories, the burden of their lives.

He clung there for an hour, until tears he didn't know he still harbored were spent. Shivering, chilled to the bone, he looked up at the waning moon and stars above. "Forgive me," he whispered through chattering teeth. "Forgive me. Oh, God, forgive me," he cried, feeling unworthy of the gifts he had been given: Life. Hope. A future.

Jared edged to the side, trying to stand on shaking legs that cramped from the cold, worried for the first time that the current might claim him. Carefully he made his way toward shore and then to the bridge. He turned on the engine and the heater, then sat there for hours just thinking, letting the image of their sacrifices wash over him like the river had washed over him. Gradually his clothes grew drier and he stopped shivering. He turned on his headlights and stared at the smooth concrete before him, reinforced by steel and sturdy enough to withstand a hundred winters.

The bridge.

His mother had crossed it, wanting to take him to something better.

The old man had saved him from it, kept it from taking his life, too.

And God, Eden's Lord, was calling him to cross it. Their combined sure belief and sacrifice helped Jared put hands and feet to all of Father Frank's lofty talks of salvation at the chapel at Buckley.

224 | Lisa Tawn Bergren

Suddenly it just *clicked.* It made sense to him. He had to make the walk. He had to take the steps if he wanted to understand what was calling to him, to his heart.

God had come near that fateful day when Anna and Ernie died. And God had come near again. Tonight. Jared could feel him all around. He just had to reach out and take his hand.

Eden pulled the truck over at the bridge the next morning, frowning. Jared's car was where he had left it, the driver's door ajar, but no one was inside. She put one boot out to the ground and stood. "Jared?" she called. "Jared!" Had something happened to him after she left? While there was little crime in the valley, there were plenty of accidents. Eden's mind flickered between the worst of possibilities.

She slammed the truck door and ran along the bridge, scanning the water beneath. Rocks covered in lime-green moss held tight to the river's bottom. *Please Lord,* she prayed, *don't let him have come to harm.* "Jared!" she called, hearing the hint of panic in her own voice. "Jared!"

"Up here!" a deep voice shouted. She turned toward the sound, her heart slowing a bit. He emerged from the birch grove on the cliff, her prayer spot. Eden's shoulders slumped in relief. "Come on," he invited. "Come up here!"

Smiling in curiosity now, she turned, left the bridge, and found the deer path. She crested the steep hill and descended toward her sacred place among the cottonwoods. Jared's light tone had quickened her heart, made her hopeful. He met her halfway, taking her hand and leading her back to the trampled grasses among the trees.

He turned to her. "Thank you for sharing this spot with me. For making me aware of it."

"Guess you adopted it, huh?"

"A couple of times. Eden, something exciting happened to me last night. Your question about me feeling healed—on the *inside*—stuck with me. After you left, I waded into the water—"

"You waded *into* the water?"

"I wanted to understand what your great-grandfather and my mother must've felt like in those last few moments. I wanted to *feel* their hurt and sorrow and fear," he said, almost wincing over the words as he pulled his hand to his chest.

She paused and stared at him. "And what did you discover?"

"For the first time I really thought through that entire horrible morning, and I mourned for them. I really mourned. I cried and I shouted at God, and I asked forgiveness for not being worthy. Then I accepted it. As the gift that it was for me." He turned and ran his hand through his hair, then turned back to her and grabbed a birch trunk in one hand. "I climbed out of the water—probably hypothermic, I was shaking so bad. I sat in my car, just thinking, thinking and staring at the bridge. Knowing it wasn't that bridge, of course, just considering all that had gone on. And Eden," he said, his eyes lighting up, "he touched me."

"Who touched you?"

"*God.* Suddenly it all made sense," Jared said excitedly, gesturing toward the air. "I think…I think for a long time I've been trying to live up to that sacrifice, working three times as hard as other people to prove I was worthy of their…lives."

"But that's impossible."

"Right. I finally discovered the truth of it last night. I'm still trying to accept it. That I'll never work hard enough to make myself worthy of their deaths. I can only live my life as fully as I can and accept the gift I was given."

She smiled with him, at the wonder of vision and the discovery of truth. They stood there for a moment, relishing it, and then Eden sobered a little. "You leave today," she stated softly, still trying to keep the smile on her face.

"Yes," he said, his face sorrowful. "I have to."

Eden nodded. "Come. I have something I want to send with you."

He followed behind her, down the path and to the truck. She leaned across the seat and took out a small crate, opening the lid as she turned. "This is for you," she said.

Jared lifted the sculpture from the straw. It was a small figure of a man, arms stretched out wide and accepting, his face turned upward, his features peaceful. He looked from it to her. "It makes me think of you that day in your prayer spot. I hope one day I can be this open."

"I think you already are," she said softly. "And this is for Nick. I won't go to the house now and get all blubbery. Just tell him I'll miss him." She lifted another sculpture from the box, that of a small boy sitting on a grassy bank, patiently waiting for the fish to bite.

"It's great. He'll love it."

"And this is to replace our pot I broke." She handed him an elegant urn, glazed a deep Swan River green.

He considered it for a long moment, turning it over with one hand to really appreciate it. "Thanks, Eden. For…for everything."

"You're welcome, Jared."

They kissed then, softly, not embracing, and then Eden climbed into her truck. Jared didn't shut her door this time, didn't say goodbye. He turned and walked with heavy steps to his car.

Eden tore her eyes away, unable to watch, to bear the tearing pain of separation. "This is of you, Lord," she chanted. She revved her engine as Jared entered his BMW and reversed, then turned away and drove off. "This is of you, Lord," she said again, trying to will the words into her heart, make right everything that felt so wrong. She turned the truck and headed home, conscious of the growing physical separation between herself and Jared as if she could feel every inch. "I pray this is of you. Please," she said through her tears, "let this be of you."

CHAPTER FIFTEEN

Jared walked through Central Park on his lunch hour, kicking at leaves of gold and rust and burnt orange, feeling as if everything was wrong. Things were on track again at the office, and he had slipped back into the pace at work more easily than he had anticipated, leaving little time for the physical exercise and spiritual pursuits he had planned all the way back to New York. He felt disquiet inside, unable to find that sense of unsurpassed peace he had discovered on the bridge in Montana. He had taken to lunchtime walks, hoping to recapture a portion of what he had found sitting in Eden's prayer spot. There were places in the park that few ever ventured into, and Jared frequently risked his two-hundred-dollar Amalfi shoes to get there.

He knew it wasn't the location that was the problem—God was everywhere. It was him. He was having trouble concentrating, keeping it all straight in his head. He had thought that, once he crossed the bridge, everything of importance would come to him easily, readily, but that was not the case. There was a deep, abiding peace in his heart now, but like the river, life went on as always, with the same challenging bends to deal with. He clung to the Truth, begging God to come nearer, to show him the way. And still, at the end of every bone-wearying day, he collapsed on the sofa in a dark, cold apartment, too tired to change out of his clothes before sleep overtook him, too weary to figure out what niggled at him.

Sitting on a boulder in the middle of Central Park, Jared took out his cell phone and dialed the Buckley Boys' Academy. "Father Frank, please," he said quietly when the operator answered. Jared had begun calling the old priest soon after dropping Nick off at school, searching for wisdom in his world.

"Jared," the old man said, as pleased to hear from him as if he had shown up in his office with a basket full of fruit.

"Father Frank," Jared said with a smile, "how's my boy?"

"Caught him throwing spitballs this morning in chapel," the man said gravely.

Jared stifled a laugh. "What'd you make him do?"

"Three pews by toothbrush."

"Ouch!" Jared said, releasing a quiet laugh. "I remember you made me do six for the same transgression when I was eight."

"Ah, yes, there's the truth of it—I'm getting soft in my old age. Or I'm a fuller representation of God's grace." He paused for a moment, then said, "Jared, the boy is fine. I think he's missing you. The summer was good; it's all he's talked about since he returned to us. But he misses you."

Jared frowned and closed his eyes. "I don't know what to do about that, Father. I work until eight most nights, sometimes ten. I can't have him sitting in an empty apartment. He's better off at Buckley."

"If that's the case, yes. But could you cut back a bit? The work will always be there, but the boy won't."

"I…I don't see how."

"Could you hire more staff?"

"Not right now."

"Could you delegate more responsibility?"

"No, not really."

"Well then, you're in a pickle, aren't you?"

"A bit."

"Jared, tell me. Is it worth it? Do you find your work fulfilling at the end of those long days?"

"Most days," he said after a moment. "For the most part." Then, "Do you?"

"Oh yes, every day. Some days are harder than others, mind you, but I've always loved my work. It's not a fair comparison, I suppose, since I get to work with children and my Lord. Not everyone can do that. And he can use you in the world of commodities, too, Jared, if that's where he wants you. He can make your heart sing with the good you do for others, the money you make that puts food on another man's table, the way you deal with others honorably." He paused a second. "You do do all that, don't you, Jared?"

Jared nodded and paced around the rock. "Yes. More and more I can see ways to live for a higher purpose. And that's good, rewarding. All in all, my life has taken a good turn. But I still feel... unsettled." There was silence on the other end. "Father Frank?"

"Yes, yes, I'm here. Just thinking. Thinking about how the good Lord keeps us on our toes. What about this woman who fishes? The woman in Montana that Nicolaus speaks of?"

"What about her?" Jared asked, guarded.

"Is she a part of your 'unsettled' feeling?"

Jared kicked at a stone in the grass, ignoring the scuff marks it left on the toe of his shoe. "I suppose. I try not to think about it."

"Why?"

"*Why?* Because it hurts too much."

"So you love her."

"Loved her. Past tense. It wasn't the right time for us. The right place."

Father Frank was silent for a moment longer. "Or perhaps it was."

Jared sighed and looked up at a light blue, autumn sky. "Thanks, Father Frank," he said quietly.

"Anytime, my boy, anytime."

Eden ran her hands over the cold surface of the latest sculpture for her exhibit, a woman tenderly cradling a one-year-old child. From the start she'd thought of it as Anna and Jared before that day on the bridge.

She could feel Renee's eyes on her from across the counter. It was a slow day in the gallery, being that it was November, after the Labor Day crowds had departed and preceding any winter visitor traffic. "I've had three offers on her already," Renee moaned.

"So you've said," Eden muttered. "She's not for sale."

"If not for sale, why show them? People respond to these pieces, Eden. They feel your heart and soul because they show through in what you've created here. They want them."

"I know," Eden said, nodding. "I'm getting there. I guess I thought the big deal was actually letting them be seen by others. Now I find that the really big deal is letting them go." She glanced at Renee. "It's like letting a piece of *me* go."

"Isn't that what artists do?" Renee asked dolefully.

Eden raised her eyebrows. "I suppose." She smiled, then said, "Guess I never felt quite so attached to my pottery before."

Renee smiled back. "You could have reproductions made. Keep the original for yourself."

"I could," Eden agreed. "I still haven't decided if that's…right. These figures," she said, pausing to again stroke the arm of the mother lovingly, "were given to me. Like visions."

"It shows," Renee said admiringly. "Do that, Eden. Keep the originals for yourself, and sell ten copies of each of them."

"What'll I do with them? They'll take up half of my attic studio."

"With what you'll make on them, you can rent a storage unit. Or buy a bigger house." She came around and stood by the mother figure with Eden. "You should've sent them to New York with Jared."

"Jared," Eden said, making his name sound like dirty laundry. "Haven't heard from him since he left. It's been more than two months. If he cares so little about me, I doubt he cares anything about my sculpture."

"So he has a few things to work out. He'll be back."

"That's what Gram keeps telling me too, but I don't think so. I don't even know if I want him to anymore." She turned and walked to the front of the gallery, staring out the window at Electric Avenue. "I ran into Julie Vose last week. She told me she had sold Rudy's place."

Eden could hear Renee suck in her breath. "I'm sorry. I thought for sure he'd be back. That he'd take it off the market."

"I think a part of me did too. Now that part tells me he's gone."

"Did you love him, Eden?" Renee asked carefully.

"Yes," she said, "I think I did."

Renee came to her then, giving her a fierce hug. "I'm proud of you, Eden. For putting yourself out there. For giving it a try."

Eden gave her a sad smile and said, "It wasn't all bad. It was a fun summer. And look at what he got me to do. If it wasn't for Jared

Conway, I wouldn't be showing these figures." She paused, thinking. "Maybe I wouldn't have been given these figures to sculpt at all."

"What does that mean?"

"I don't know. It's like I've always thought of this mother sculpture as Anna Conway, holding her baby in her arms." She looked at the other two statues. "Maybe they're all of her. Jared gave me a part of her, helped me see her. He helped me see *me* better."

"So you don't want to kill him for leaving?"

She shook her head. "I don't want to kill him. I'm too sad to be angry. I want to curl up in his arms and cry for what we could've had. I want to feel him holding me and know that he's feeling the same kind of hurt. Isn't that crazy? I want to know I'm not alone, even if it just makes us both miserable."

Jared ran his fingers down the smooth glaze of the urn Eden had given him, then picked up the figure he kept on his desk. He leaned over and buzzed Don over the intercom. "Hey. Want to have dinner with me tonight?"

"I dunno. I'm pretty attached to my frozen pizza repertoire. Last night was sausage, the night before pepperoni—"

"I'll buy."

"I'm there. What time?"

"Eight?"

"Eight it is, my man."

Jared released the intercom button and picked up the sculpture again. He walked over to the big picture window that met on two sides of his office, considering all he had worked for over the years, all he had accomplished. He had the thousand-dollar, ergonomically perfect chair, the handcrafted mahogany desk, the offices in a pricey high-rise. He had clients with famous names. He had expensive shoes and tailored suits. He had a nice flat that Patricia was living in, as well as a nice flat for himself.

But what he wanted was a home. He wanted his son nearby. He wanted to jog over to Eden's. He wanted the peace on the figure's face.

Jared held his head in his hand, staring and staring at the sculpture in his other palm. It was then that the realization of all he had, all he wanted, swept over him.

"Miss Tenney?" he called.

His secretary peered through the doorway a second later.

"Get a real estate agent on the phone for me, would you? Julie Vose. Bigfork, Montana. Then I want to talk to my ex-wife."

"Yes sir," Miss Tenney said slowly, as if she were thinking her job might be in jeopardy if the boss was thinking about a return trip to Montana.

Jared smiled and turned back to his stack of papers, but he had difficulty concentrating. A moment later, Miss Tenney's voice sounded over the intercom. "Ms. Vose on the phone for you, sir."

"Thanks. Hello? Julie?"

"Yes. How are you, Mr. Conway?"

"I'm fine. No. More than fine. Say, you never did tell me about the couple who bought Rudy's old place."

"Oh, that was a couple from town," she said slowly. "They wanted a getaway cabin on the water. They were thrilled with what you had done with the place. Just right for them."

Jared smiled. "See if you can't make them a deal, would you? Tell them I want it back. That I'll pay them ten thousand dollars more for their trouble. An investment, they can call it."

"You want to buy it back? After all you went through to sell it?"

"After all I went through to sell it, I finally realized I shouldn't have sold it at all." He lowered his voice. "Do you think you can get it back for me, Julie? It's important."

"I don't know," she said. "They were pretty excited. And they said it was just perfect... Are you sure you want to do this? Why don't you come out, and I'll show you a few other properties? A few with some acreage or something in a different price range?"

"I'm sure there are a lot of beautiful homes, Julie. I saw a couple of them. Maybe even something that would be better for me and my son. But I want Rudy's place. It became home to us. It's important," he repeated.

"Well, all right. I'll give them a call and see what they say. You can still be reached at the same numbers I had last spring?"

"Those same numbers. Thank you. Oh, and Julie?"

"Yes?"

"Can you look up the elementary school administrator's number in Bigfork for me?" He listened as she rifled through the narrow Flathead County phone book and then listed off the numbers. "Thanks."

"My pleasure, Mr. Conway."

Seconds later, Miss Tenney buzzed him again. "Your ex-wife's on the phone, sir."

"Thanks." He pressed another flashing button. "Patricia? Are you free for lunch tomorrow?"

"Yes," she said, a bit slowly and suspiciously. He had spoken little to her since she had picked up Nick from Montana and flown home. Jared smiled, thinking of how weary she had looked when he showed up in town three days later, already tired of her mother role. Last month she had called to say she couldn't make Buckley's parents' weekend because she was "going out of town."

"Can you join me at that sandwich place we used to go to down the street?"

"Yes," she said slowly. "May I ask what this is about?"

"It's better if we talk about it in person. Say noon?"

"Noon at the corner," she agreed.

He hung up the phone and stared at it for a moment, then forced himself to try to concentrate on the work at hand. If he was about to do what he thought he was about to do, there was a lot to get done.

Jared picked up his glass in a toast and waited for Don to do the same. "To the business."

"To the business," his friend said, smiling and raising his glass. He sipped, then set the goblet down and dug into his chicken parmesan once more. "It's good to have you back," he said, his mouth half full. "For a while I thought you weren't coming back at all."

"For a while *I* thought about not coming back," Jared allowed.

"And then I screwed things up in July," Don said, smiling, far enough past the trauma to laugh about it, "and I saw how fast you got your hidey-ho back here, and *wham,* I knew there was no getting the business out of Jared Conway's blood. You're in it for good, baby."

"Maybe."

"What? Maybe? You're not kiddin' this boy, bud. You love what we do. The homework, the guesswork, the victories. Even the occasional loss. It thickens the pot—makes it that much sweeter when you win."

"Uh-huh," Jared agreed, "I have loved all of that."

Don eyed him suspiciously. "So. What are we celebrating tonight?"

"Your business." Jared let the words roll off his tongue, wondering how he could be doing what he was doing, yet knowing it was exactly right.

"Well, I've brought in some new accounts lately, but—"

"No, Don." Jared waited until his partner finished chewing and set down his fork. "I want you to buy me out. I want out. I want to leave it with you."

Abruptly Don stopped breathing, let alone chewing. Then he choked.

Jared looked around in embarrassment and stooped over the table to thump his partner on the back. "You okay?"

Don nodded, his face red. After a moment, a sip of water, he sat back and stared at his friend. "Why? After all this time? We're finally where we wanted to be fifteen years ago when we started. And now you want out?"

"And now I want out. It was a good fifteen years, Don. But I've missed too much. I missed my son's first eight years. I missed love. I missed life."

Don shook his head, uncomprehending. "But you love what we do."

"I have. Now I'm going to find out what else I love."

"Are you moving? Is this about that woman?"

Jared considered his words and then bobbed his head once. "It's about Eden, yes."

"Oh, *Eden…*" Don said.

"But it's more about me. I went on that trip, Don, and it changed me. After all those years, I found out that I hadn't laid my mother's memories to rest, let alone all the important things a man has to deal with."

"So you're going to chuck it all and move across country? Sell the biz, rent your flat, and just go? I mean, I assume you're heading back—back to Montana."

"I think so." Again, the words left his mouth and Jared wondered at the power of them. The power of decision.

"Sounds like a midlifer to me."

"No, Don. This is the real thing. This is a new life begun."

Eden smiled as she watched the sunset to the west, and the reflection on the snowcapped Swan Range to the east. The fish weren't biting—they usually didn't on this calm stretch of river—but she didn't care. She was left with the peaceful *whir* of the line as it passed her ear, the scent of decomposing wood, and the silt of the receding shoreline.

The water was nearly still, making a perfect mirror for the incredible pink-and-white mountains before her. The trees along either side of the river were in their last days of their change, seeming to sense that the snow on the mountains high above was soon to overtake them too. The last vestiges of summer were most assuredly gone now, leaving Eden feeling a bit melancholy, as it always did. She liked each of the seasons in the valley, but this past summer had been special—sacred. She would always remember it fondly. As the summer that love had found her.

Despite the fact it hadn't lasted. Like the vision of an osprey swooping down to the water as its claws pierced a trout for dinner, Eden was getting to the place where she could appreciate the beauty of what had transpired in spite of the tragedy at the end. Life was full of disappointments. The trick was to find the divine appointments— that was what pulled Eden through. And in retrospect, her summer had been full of them.

Across the river a beaver slid down the bank, its wide tail plastering the brown and fading reedy grass in place, just as it had perhaps a hundred times before. He surfaced twenty feet out, swimming downriver to where the trees were young and strong and not so thick that a guy with buckteeth couldn't bring them home. They were building a dam on the inlet across from her, he and his mate, about fifteen yards upriver, preparing for winter and a den full of kits come spring. Again Eden felt a pang of loneliness, but she pushed it away, concentrating on the beauty, the perfection of the moment. "Thank you, Lord," she whispered, perfectly setting Ernie's fly—an ancient, blue-and-green Spanner—near a graying snag that just might harbor a hungry trout. The old rod was still good, even after all these years.

The trout bit a second later, hungry, ready. Eden moved toward the ancient, dead tree, watching as the fish ran, fighting the line. Quickly she yanked backward, setting the hook before he freed himself, and slowly brought him in. Once on the muddy bank, she sat beside the twenty-six inch long rainbow, admiring the reflection of the evening light in his shiny gills as she unhooked him and set him free. "Live life to its fullest this winter, my friend," she said to him, his mouth opening and closing, desperate for the river, " 'cause next year it might not be catch and release."

She stood and eased him back into the river, watching as the water stilled. The fish was on his side, sucking in water, taking life from it, then suddenly he righted himself and swam away. Eden smiled and turned the old Spanner in her hand, admiring one of many flies her great-grandfather had tied himself. He had been a craftsman, an artist when it came to tying the delicate Nymph or the more gaudy Green Drake, and a master of everything between. She could imagine him as an old man, laboring with arthritic, thick fingers on the tiny strands that would one day bring in fish after fish.

She sighed and stared out at the ever-changing river before her, now reflecting an ethereal salmon pink and lavender. Her great-grandfather had lived his last days at the river's edge, eaten from its depths, left his life on the muddy bank. Her eyes turned toward the old rod she held in her hands, wondering about the day Ernie had last held it, before it was discarded in an effort to save a young woman and her child. She thought about her great-grandmother's confusion and grief in discovering his body on the bank and a young life in his arms. A boy who would one day return. She considered the moment when Ernie might have known he would not see another sunrise on the Swan or feel the joy of holding his wife's hand in his or experience the peace of one perfect cast to the sweet spot the trout favored. She wondered about the moment he saw Jesus, with his arms open wide, welcoming him.

And Eden wept as she smiled.

Epilogue

Nick was waiting for him with Father Frank when Jared drove up the long, winding, perfectly paved road to Buckley. The boy, backpack already on, ran toward him, then alongside the car as Jared pulled to a stop. Jared got out laughing, and bending down, welcomed his son with a fierce embrace.

He rose and shook the priest's hand.

"The papers are all taken care of," the older man said. "There are a few things we'll send you, but all is in order."

"I can't believe I'm leaving," Nicolaus said. " 'Bye, Father Frank!" Quickly he hopped in Jared's BMW and slammed the door.

Jared and the old priest laughed together. "Think he's afraid you'll leave him behind."

"Never. Never again," Jared promised, staring into his eyes.

They shook hands again, and then Father Frank pulled him close for a warm hug. "It's a fine thing you're doing, my boy. You're making the right decision. I feel it in my soul."

"I know," Jared said, amazed at the assuredness in his own heart. "Ready?" he asked his son through the glass.

Nicolaus gave him the thumbs-up sign.

"Thanks for everything, Father. For...everything."

"It was my pleasure, Jared. Go with God."

"I intend to," Jared said, walking to his side of the car. "We'll keep in touch."

"Please. I'd like that."

"Me, too. Good-bye."

"Good-bye, Jared." Father Frank bent to knock on Nick's window. "Take care of your dad, boy. He's out of practice again."

"I will," Nicolaus promised solemnly. "'Bye!"

Jared turned the key in the ignition and reached for the Rand McNally map book. "Here," he said, handing it to his son. "Find Montana for me."

Dear Friends,

Thank you for reading the book of my heart, *The Bridge*. I don't know if it's because the novel is set in an area of the country I love or because it was inspired by a song that tugged at my heartstrings from the get-go, but I really enjoyed writing this novel! I've spent every summer of my life on Swan Lake, so you've just entered into a part of my life that few people get to see. (My parents don't invite just anyone to their teeny, tiny cabin.)

My family and I are doing well. Olivia is preparing for first grade, and Emma was ready for preschool about the time she turned one. She won't get to ride the school bus like her big sister Liv, but she'll go a couple of times a week, giving Mama more opportunities to write. My husband, Tim, is enjoying a flourishing business. If you're curious, his work can be seen at *www.bergrendesign.com*. He's quite the impressive sculptor, in my unbiased opinion.

I hope you enjoyed reading *The Bridge,* from Eden's decision to risk to Jared's investigation of what sacrifice really means—and God's love affair with them both. I have posted a reader's guide for this novel on my Web site, should your discussion group care to read my book. You may find it at *www.lisatawnbergren.com*.

Wishing you every blessing,

Lisa Tawn Bergren

Write to Lisa Tawn Bergren:
c/o WaterBrook Press
2375 Telstar Drive, Suite 160
Colorado Springs, CO 80920

If you enjoyed *The Bridge*,
look for Lisa Tawn Bergren's next book,
Christmas Every Morning
Available Fall 2002

In a New Mexico nursing home, patiently awaiting death, sits Charlotte Mueller, a woman who long ago retreated behind the silent wall of Alzheimer's. But Cimarron Canyon Care Center's director, Dane McConnell, is researching the effects of Christmas rooms. As part of his study, the center has set aside one room that remains decorated for the holidays 365 days a year. Each day when Charlotte visits the Christmas room, she sings entire carols from memory—and soon the woman who has been unreachable for years resurfaces.

Dane calls Charlotte's estranged daughter, Krista Mueller, with the news that Charlotte is suffering from congestive heart failure and does not have long to live. Dane knows Krista will want to come and say good-bye, regardless of the abyss between mother and daughter. And there's something more he wants to share with her. A nurse's aide has discovered a Christmas journal among Charlotte's things, a journal that documents a life fully lived, if forgotten—a life full of regrets and hopes and joys and sorrows. Paging through it, Dane realizes the importance of helping Krista discover this part of her mother's history, of giving her the chance to hear Charlotte sing once more before she dies. But the clock is ticking...